New TOEIC Listening Script

auditor n. 旁聽者、查帳員   obey v. 服從
audition n. 聽力、試唱、演、試聽   <u>obedient</u> adj. 順從的
audit v. 旁聽 n. 查帳   ↳ *disobedient*
                                          to hear

PART 1

1. (C) (A) Some people are in a bank.
     (B) Some people are in a lobby.
     (C) Some people are in a restaurant.
     (D) Some people are in an <u>auditorium</u>. 聽眾席 (UP) place
          hear   禮堂

2. (C) (A) The boys are seated {sitting} to the left of the woman.
     (B) The boys are hugging to the right of the woman. 擁抱
     (C) The boys are fighting in front of the woman. 打架
     (D) The boys are laughing behind the woman. 笑

3. (D) (A) The car has a <u>siren</u> on its <u>roof</u>. 車頂上有汽笛、警報器
     (B) The truck has a <u>crane</u> <u>mounted</u> on the back. 卡車有起重機架在後面
     (C) The train has a section for smokers. → mount 架、架置
     (D) The bus has a <u>rack</u> for bicycles. ⊙爬上 ⊕上馬
          火車有區給抽煙者的   架子
          → They mounted a small hill.

4. (B) (A) Some people are swimming in a pond. 池塘
     (B) Some people are sitting in <u>cubicles</u>. 小隔間
     (C) Some people are standing in line. cubicle coma
     (D) Some people are lying in bed. waiting
          隔間昏迷：一上班就精神不濟

5. (D) (A) The woman is holding some books. 抱著一些書
     (B) The woman is washing some clothes. 洗衣服
     (C) The woman is reading to some children. 念書給孩子聽
     (D) The woman is working with some <u>bricks</u>.
          在處理一些磚頭、磚塊

6. (B) (A) The man is painting a wall. 擦牆壁油漆
     (B) The man is replacing a light bulb. 更換燈泡
     (C) The man is testing a <u>smoke detector</u>. 測試煙霧探測器
     (D) The man is grilling a steak. 烤牛排
          grill v. ①烤 ②拷問 <u></u> n. 烤架
          → She was grilled for 24 hours at the police station.

U0084650

GO ON TO THE NEXT PAGE.

45

PART 2

這個貨是誰簽收的?

7. (A) Who signed for the delivery?
    (A) Ms. Harris.
    n. 投遞、交付.
    (B) May 22th.
    (C) Seventy-five dollars.

* slippery adj.
① 滑的
② 靠不住的 He is a slippery character.
（他是個靠不住的人）
③ 不穩定的 That is a slippery situation
④ 需小心對待的, 棘手的
a slippery economic problem

我應該把冷氣打開嗎?

8. (B) Should I turn on the air conditioning?
    (A) The floor looks slippery. 地板看起來滑滑的
    (B) Yes, it's hot in here.
    (C) With cream and sugar, please.

* booth   n. 有篷的貨攤
/buθ/   (美)公用電話亭

你的攤子會在農夫市集的哪裡呢?

9. (A) Where will your booth be at the farmer's market?
    (A) Near the north exit. 靠近北出口
    (B) There's nothing left. 沒有剩下東西
    (C) Before the growing season. 在生長季之前

* empty adj. ① 空的, 未佔用的
= unoccupied
= vacant

辦公室今天感覺空空的

10. (A) The office feels empty today.
    (A) Several staff members are absent.
    (B) No, I told her to come early.
    (C) The weekly weather forecast.

② 缺少 + of
His words are empty of sincerity.
他的文字缺乏誠意

每週氣象預報

* absent adj. ① 缺席的

11. (A) When did we last update our website?
    (A) Last week. 我們最後更新網頁是何
    (B) Yes, I read that this morning. 時?
    (C) The paint isn't dry yet. 油漆還沒乾

② 缺少的: Snow is absent in his country
③ 心不在焉的: He has an absent look
                on his face.

誰會出現在我們下次的化妝品廣告宣傳活動?

* appear
v. 出現, 演出. 似乎

12. (B) Who's appearing in our next cosmetics ad campaign?
    (A) They'll be shot on location. 外景拍攝
    (B) A world-famous supermodel. 世界著名的超模
    (C) Here's a pen that works. 這是可以用的筆

appear { that
      { to V

他的政策提案被拒絕時他是如何反應的?

* reject

13. (B) How did Mr. Finch react when his policy proposal was rejected?
    (A) Everyone except Rondell. 每個人除了 Rondell
    (B) He was discouraged, of course. 他當然很沮喪
    (C) In last week's financial forecast.

v. 拒絕, 丟棄, 駁回, 排斥
→ All apples with soft spots
    were rejected.

上週的財務預報

早上或是下午的飛機去 Tampa 呢?

14. (A) Do you want the morning or the afternoon flight to Tampa? His plea was rejected.
    (A) Let me check my schedule.
    (B) The café across the street. 對街的咖啡廳
    (C) Just once a week. 一週一次

→ The patient's body rejected
the heart transplant.
病人的身體排斥心臟移植

15. (C) The Internet is working now, isn't it? 網路現在可以用了.是嗎?

    (A) I like the logo, too.

    * issue v. 發行.發佈.配給,核發
    n. 問題.爭論.爭議.期刊

    (B) I already had some. 我已經吃過一些了

    (C) No, I'm still having issues. 不.我仍然有些問題

16. (B) Can you take a look at the schedule for next week? 你可以看一下下週的行程表嗎?

    (A) It's in a convenient location. 是個方便的地點

    (B) Sure, I'll do it in a minute. 好.我馬上做

    (C) By overnight delivery? 隔日到貨嗎?

    * in a minute
    in a little while
    in a second
    in a short time
    in due time
    in short order

17. (A) Why have they blocked off Taylor Street? 為何他們要隔開泰勒街

    (A) A water main burst. 自來水總管 burst 爆炸

    (B) Only two blocks. 只有兩個街區

    (C) No, I don't believe it's true.

    * transfer v.
    A→B 「carry
    搬、轉換.調動

18. (C) Hasn't the delivery truck been loaded yet? 運貨卡車還沒有裝貨嗎?

    (A) That option is best. 那個選項最好

    (B) Sure, I'll download that program. 我會下載那個程式

    (C) No, some items had to be repackaged. 有些商品需要重新包裝

19. (C) Fiona Oliver was transferred to a different department, wasn't she? Fiona Oliver 被調到不同的部門.是嗎?

    (A) The driver is on his way. 駕駛在路上

    (B) The appliances are all new. 設備是全新的

    (C) Yes, she's in Marketing now. 在行銷部門

20. (B) How do I access the hotel's business center? 我要如何進到飯店的商務中心

    (A) It's 25 dollars per day. 一天25元

    (B) Use your hotel key card. 用你的飯店房卡

    (C) No, I don't think it does. 我不覺得這個可以

    * permit
    permit v. 允許
    permit n. 許可證
    to apply for a permit
    申請許可證

21. (C) I'm thinking about attending the professional development seminar. 我在想,去參加專業發展研討會

    (A) Take a left at the corner. 在轉角處左轉

    (B) October 20th and 27th.

    (C) I personally found it very helpful. 我個人覺得這非常有幫助

22. (A) Do you think it's OK to park my car here for now? 你覺得我現在把車停在這裡可以嗎?

    (A) The sign says "By permit only." 標示說:有許可證才可停

    (B) That's a dangerous part of town. 那是鎮上危險的地方

    (C) Just three minutes. 只有三分鐘

GO ON TO THE NEXT PAGE

23. (B) Which restaurant are we taking our clients to this evening? 今天晚上我們要帶客戶去哪間餐廳?
    (A) Sure, thanks! 當然,謝謝
    (B) I thought we had reservations at Tribeca Bistro. 我想我們在 Tribeca 小餐館有預約
    (C) Usually around 8 o'clock. 通常8點左右

24. (A) Where's the Kimball Theater?
    (A) There's a floor plan near the elevator. 電梯旁有樓層佈置圖
    (B) I moved to a different room. 我搬到不同的房間
    (C) Lee's presentation is after mine. Lee的演講在我之後

    *presentation
    n. 上演,展演,提出
    → The presentation of evidence. 提出證據

25. (C) Who do you recommend for legal services? 你推薦誰做法律服務?
    (A) We can pay by credit card. 可以用信用卡付款
    (B) Their fees have nearly doubled. 他們的費用接近2倍
    (C) I need to find someone as well. 我也需要找某人 (也需要找做法律服務的人)

    nearly 幾乎,差不多
    也

26. (A) When do you finish work today? 你今天何時做完工作(何時下班)
    (A) Well, I still have a lot to do. 嗯~我還有很多要做(沒那麼早下班)
    (B) Does Steve also work there? Steve也在這裡工作嗎?
    (C) He was in the conference room. 他在會議室裡頭

27. (C) Are you serious about finding a new job? 對於找新工作這事你是認真的嗎?
    (A) Some computer consultants. 電腦顧問
    (B) The monthly budget report. 每月的預算報告
    (C) Yeah, I'm done here. 我在這裡的任務完成了

    I'm done! 我做好了,我吃過了
    = Finished.
    I'm finished. 我完成了

28. (A) Why did Ms. Wrightwood cancel the product launch? 他為何取消新品推出(商品)發表
    (A) Actually, she just pushed it back a week. 事實上,他只是推遲一週
    (B) What time is our flight? 我們的飛機幾點?
    (C) I'd like the next available opening.

    would like 想要
    開頭,開幕,空缺,職缺

29. (C) Could you take the late shift for me tomorrow evening? 你明天晚上可以替我上晚班嗎?
    (A) Just leave it here. 放在這兒就可以了
    (B) Yes, it is getting cold outside. 對,外面變冷了
    (C) Sorry, I have tickets to the baseball game. 我有棒球賽的票

    *shift
    n. 轉換,轉移,手段,輪班
    → The lazy man tried every shift to avoid doing his work.

30. (C) How much will it cost to send these packages? 寄這個包裹要花多少錢?
    (A) About seven days. 大約7天
    (B) This type of packaging, please. 這種包裝 麻煩
    (C) When do you want them to arrive? 你想要何時寄到?

31. (A) Have you printed out my itinerary? 我的行程資料印出來了嗎? itinerary
　　(A) I thought you wanted to reschedule two meetings.
　　(B) Round trip tickets are expensive. 我以為你想要重新安排 n. 路線、
　　(C) Helen is taking his place. 來回票是貴的. 2個會議. 旅行計量
　Helen 取代他的位置　　　　　　　　　　　　　　　　　adj. 旅程的
　　　　　　　　　　take sb's place 取代某人　　　　　　路線的 + map

PART 3

Questions 32 through 34 refer to the following conversation.

/lu'tenant/ n.中尉、少尉　　　　河邊警察局打來　　　我這裡看到你會

M : Hello, this is Lieutenant Vance calling from the Riverside Police Department. I see here that
you will be bringing your students to the station for a tour and first-aid demonstration. Do
最後確認數目 you have a final count of how many people, students and guardians, will be coming?

W : Yes, we'll be 32 people in total. I can email you a list of names later today.
　　　　　　　　　今天晚一點可以 mail 出所有人名單給你

M : Perfect! That way, we can print up some personalized visitor badges for each one of you.
　　　　這樣一來, 我們可以印些個人化的參觀章給你們每一個人。

32. (A) Where does the man work?
　　(A) At a police station.　　　　　　* first-aid 急救的、急救
　　(B) At a school library.　　　　　　+ demonstration 演示
　　(C) At a transportation company. 運輸公司　　+ kit 急救箱
　　(D) At a theater. ↳ public transportation　+ material 急救用品
　　　　　　　　　　　　　　　　　　　　　+ officer 急救員

33. (C) What does the man ask about? 公司在哪裡
　　(A) When a meeting will start.
　　(B) Where a business is located. 公司在哪裡
　　(C) How many visitors are expected. 預計有多少人 * badge n. 徽章、標記
　　(D) How the bill will be paid. 帳單如何付　　Wisdom is the badge of
　　　　　　　　　　　　　　　　　　　　　　matunity.

34. (B) What will the man prepare?　　智慧是成熟的象徵
　　(A) Informational brochures. 資訊手冊
　　(B) Name badges.
　　(C) Training manuals. 訓練手冊
　　(D) An expense report. 支出報告

Questions 35 through 37 refer to the following conversation.

W : This is Ashley Earl speaking. 尖塔　　　打來關於你運到的包裹

M : Ms. Earl, this is Willie Spires from SkyHigh Airlines. I'm calling about your delayed baggage.
It has finally arrived at the airport and I can have it sent to you this afternoon.
很高興知道(真是好消息)　　　可以把包裹寄給你
W : That's good to know, but I won't be home this afternoon. Could you possibly leave the
suitcase by the front door of my house? 你有可能把行李箱放在我家前門嗎?

GO ON TO THE NEXT PAGE

M : I'm afraid we need someone to sign for it so we can make sure it's been delivered.

恐怕需要有人簽收，我們才能確定物品已經送到。

W : Well, how about leaving it with my next door neighbor? He frequently signs for my deliveries. He's retired and home during the day. I can call him and let him know you're coming.

→嗯，那把東西給我隔壁鄰居如何？他常常把我簽收。他退休了，而且白天都在家，我可以打給他告知你們要來

35. (A) What is the purpose of the telephone call? 訴求意圖
    (A) To arrange a delivery.
    (B) To request an upgrade. 要求更新(升等)
    (C) To place an order. 下訂單
    (D) To confirm a reservation. 確認預約

通訊軟體簡稱意法補充

afk : away from keyboard 不在位置上
→ I have to be afk for a meeting and will be back in 30 minutes.

36. (C) What does the man say is required? 他說什麼是必須的
    (A) A passport.
    (B) A credit card.
    (C) A signature.
    (D) A security code.

adj. 必須的
v. require
需要 + v-ing / that

tbd = to be determined 待確認
→ The decision is tbd since we still need some critical information.

37. (D) Who does the woman say she will call?
    (A) Her lawyer. 律師
    (B) Her boss. 老闆
    (C) Her husband. 老公
    (D) Her neighbor. 鄰居

fYI = for your information
供你參考. 順帶一提

rsvp : please reply
→ The conference meeting is set, rsvp by tonight.

Questions 38 through 40 *refer to the following conversation between three speakers.*

我昨晚在你們餐廳用餐. 我想我可能把信用卡留在桌上了

M : Excuse me, I had dinner in your restaurant last night and I think I may have left my credit card at the table.

讓我問問 Rachel   她是昨晚的值班經理

Woman UK : Hmm... OK. Let me check with Rachel. She was the supervising manager on duty last night.

supervise v. 監督. 管理

希望卡片沒被丟到垃圾桶

M : I'd appreciate it. I really hope the card didn't get thrown in the trash.

Woman UK : I doubt it... Oh, here she is. Hey, Rachel. A customer thinks he may have left his credit card at his table last night. Anything turn up? 有任何事發生嗎？(有發現卡片嗎?)

Woman US : Oh, we did find a card last night. May I have your name, sir?

M : It's Phil Robertson, and the card is an Urbanbank Visa.

鎖在   保險箱   經理的辦公室   我去拿.

Woman US : That's it. I have it locked in the safe in the manager's office. I'll go get it.

38. (D) Where are the speakers?
    (A) At a shoe store.
    (B) At a print shop. 印刷店
    (C) At a dry cleaner. 乾洗店
    (D) At a restaurant.

* I doubt it.
= I don't think so.

*turn up
①出現
②(股票.股市)
上揚.反彈. 升值

39. (C) Why is the man at the restaurant?
    (A) To return some equipment. 交還一些設備
    (B) To pick up some samples. 拿些試用品
    (C) To look for a missing item. 找尋遺失的物品
    (D) To discuss a catering order. 討論一筆外燴訂單

大通訊軟體縮寫
fwd / fw = forward
Since the email is highly
confidential, don't fwd
to other people.

40. (D) What does Rachel ask about?
    (A) A price. 價格
    (B) A color. 顏色
    (C) A location. 地點
    (D) A name. 名字

CC = carbon copy 副本
etc. et cetera = and so forth
RIP. rest in peace 安息

Questions 41 through 43 _refer to the following conversation._

對於服務是否滿意

M : Hi, this is Greg from Clearview Window and Door Company. We installed new window
blinds in your house last month. I'm calling to find out if you're satisfied with the service
you received. 整體而言,服務很滿意 be pleased with 滿意 一開始沒貨

W : Overall, I'm pleased with the service, but the blinds I ordered were originally out of stock.
That caused a delay, but when the blinds became available, your guys did a great job.

M : I'm glad to hear you're satisfied with our service. And I see in my records that your original
purchase included a 10 percent discount for first-time customers? 首購客戶有打9折

W : Um…not to my knowledge. I paid the full amount. 我不知道,我付了全額

M : That was a mistake on our end. I'll process a 10 percent refund and send a check right away.
最終是我們的錯(本質上是我們的錯)

41. (B) Why is the man calling? 確認付款資訊
    (A) To confirm payment information.
    (B) To request customer feedback. 要求客戶回饋
    (C) To offer a free consultation. 提供免費諮詢
    (D) To reschedule an installation. 重新安排安裝

at one's wit's end 全然不知所措
→ It's at my wit's end to know
what to do with my dog.

42. (B) What caused a delay? 錯過了場預約
    (A) An appointment was missed.
    (B) A product was temporarily unavailable. 暫時也不可取得
    (C) Some equipment was faulty. 有些設備有缺陷
    (D) Some forms were misplaced. 有些表格放錯了

reach the end of one's rope
山窮水盡,智窮力竭
on one's beem-ends
秤杆
經濟拮据,無所有

43. (D) What does the man say he will do?
    (A) Send some product samples.
    (B) Inspect some merchandise. 檢查些商品
    (C) Pass on some information. 傳遞些資訊
    (D) Issue a refund. 核發一個退款(發出)

× to one's knowledge
就某人所知

GO ON TO THE NEXT PAGE ➡

Questions 44 through 46 *refer to the following conversation between three speakers.*

W : Hi, I just moved into the building and I'm interested in joining your fitness center. Could you give me a brief overview of the facility?

Man UK : Of course. We're open seven days a week, 24 hours a day. In addition to free classes, members have access to indoor basketball and tennis courts, exercise equipment, and a swimming pool.

W : Exactly what I'm looking for. Is there a discount for tenants of the building?

Man UK : Ah... I'm not sure. Joe, are we still offering the tenant discount?

Man US : Yes, as long as you can prove residency, you'll be eligible for a 50 percent discount on your first year of membership.

W : Umm... I just moved in, so I don't have anything except a copy of my lease. Will that work?

Man US : Sure.

W : Great! So I'd like to sign up today. Do I just need to fill out an application?

Man UK : Yes, I have one right here.

44. (C) Where are the speakers?
   (A) At a university library.
   (B) At a train station.
   (C) At a fitness center.
   (D) At a sports stadium.

45. (D) Why does the woman need to verify her residency?
   (A) To vote in an election.
   (B) To make a reservation.
   (C) To verify her date of birth.
   (D) To receive a discount.

46. (A) What will the woman most likely do next?
   (A) Complete some paperwork.
   (B) Make an online payment.
   (C) Speak to a manager.
   (D) Sign a lease.

Questions 47 through 49 *refer to the following conversation.*

W : Though it took a long time to come up with the shape of this energy drink bottle, I think our clients will be happy with the design. It's very attractive.

M : I agree. Moreover, it's made entirely from recycled materials, which is just what the client requested.

52

W : Right. I'm pleased that everything is going so well. 我很開心事情進行得如此順利

M : Me too. Hey... a quick question. You know, I play on the company softball team, right? Well, we have a tournament starting on Friday. Would it be OK if I leave early that afternoon? 我們週五開始有個錦標賽 · 那天下午我可以早點離開嗎？

W : Well, we still have to work on the label for the bottle, but I think we can spare you for a couple of hours on Friday.

* spare v. ① 分出. 騰出
Can you spare me a few minutes?

47. (A) What are the speakers working on? 說話者他們在從事什麼(在做什麼)?
(A) A bottle design.
(B) A tax audit. 稅務稽查
(C) An advertising budget. 廣告預算
(D) A training manual. 訓練手冊

② 節省 (常用於否定. 疑問)
Spare the rod, spoil the child.
③ 饒恕, They took his money but spared his life.

48. (B) What does the man say about the company softball team? 壘球隊 (和棒球比. 球大. 棒小) 場地小
(A) The team is receiving an award. 團隊得獎
(B) The team is participating in a competition. 參加一個比賽
(C) The players are male and female. 有男生和女生
(D) The players are getting new uniforms. 得到新制服

49. (C) Why does the woman say, "I think we can spare you for a couple of hours on Friday"? 延長一個即將到來的截止日期
+ 可N.
extend v. 延長   approach v. 接近 靠近
(A) To extend an approaching deadline.
(B) To disagree with a colleague's opinion. 不同意同事的意見
(C) To approve the man's request. 同意這個人的要求
(D) To express dissatisfaction with the client's request. 對於客戶的要求表達不滿

nook 角落, cranny 裂縫
every now and then 時不時
every nook and cranny 到處

Questions 50 through 52 refer to the following conversation.

W : Thanks for meeting me in the café today, Kyle. I think it's nice to get out of the office every now and then. Plus, I like to meet with new employees in a more casual setting. So, how's everything going? 我正要繳交我的第一份顧客調查報告 環境. 安裝

M : Everything is great, Maryanne. I'm just about to submit my first consumer survey report, and I'd appreciate your feedback. I had trouble finding enough customers willing to volunteer for the survey in order to get a wide enough range of responses. 為了 得到足夠寬廣的回應(足夠多的) → 參加者很難獲得

W : Unfortunately, survey participants can be difficult to secure. Did you use our company's online database? It has a list of names of our recent customers. I find that new customers are the most willing to participate in surveys. 線上資料庫 我發現新客較願意 參加調查

GO ON TO THE NEXT PAGE

50. (D) Why did the woman want to meet with the man?
    (A) To follow up on a job offer. 跟進一個職位
    (B) To congratulate the man on a nomination.
    (C) To return a favor. 回饋好意. (回報)
    (D) To ask the man about his progress at work.
        n. 進度

(right margin notes)
nominate v.提名
nomination n.
nominator n.提名者
nominee n.被提名者
nominal adj.名義上的
ignominy n.可恥的行為
no | name

51. (B) What does the man say he had trouble with?
    (A) Submitting a report. 交報告
    (B) Finding volunteers for a survey. 找自願者做
    (C) Formatting a website. 為網站編格式 調查
    (D) Receiving international shipments.
        收國際貨運

52. (C) What does the woman suggest the man do?
    (A) Read a company handbook. 看公司手冊
    (B) Participate in a training session. 參加訓練活動
    (C) Use a database. 用資料庫
    (D) Talk to a coordinator. 和協調者聊聊

(right margin notes)
handbook
manual
guide-book
booklet
brochure

Questions 53 through 55 *refer to the following conversation.*

be able to

M : I've got good news, Betty. I was able to book Rolling Jams to perform at our club on April 17th.
把他們加到4月音樂家表演行程海報上

W : That is good news! I love those guys. I'll add them to the musician schedule on the April poster.
聽眾. 關於海報事 謝謝你做的.   你的設計很棒

M : Listen, about the poster. Thanks for doing it, by the way. Your design is perfect. But I'm just wondering about printing in black and white. Shouldn't we print in color?

W : We should, but color printing is going to be way more expensive.
→沒錯呀(我們應該)但是彩色列印會貴很多

M : Eh... I'll take a look at a budget and I'll let you know if we can afford it.
我會看一下預算

我又是在想關於黑白印刷
這件事. 我們不應該印彩色的嗎

53. (C) What is scheduled for April 17?
    (A) A board meeting. 董事會
    (B) A cooking demonstration. 廚藝展示
    (C) A musical performance. 音樂表演
    (D) A fitness center reopening. 健身中心重新開幕

54. (A) What does the man thank the woman for?
    (A) Creating a poster.
    (B) Revising a calendar. revise 修訂. 校訂一個日曆
    (C) Booking an artist. 預約一個藝術家(表演者)
    (D) Responding to a complaint. 回應一個抱怨

(right margin notes)
* complaint n.
complain v.

55. (C) What does the man say he will do?
 (A) Contact a print shop. 聯絡一間印刷店
 (B) Listen to a recording. 聽一個錄音
 (C) Check a budget. 看看預算
 (D) Update a schedule. 更新行程

contact v.
contact n. 接觸, 碰觸, 熟人
→ He made contacts with wealthy people in raising money for the project.

Questions 56 through 58 refer to the following conversation. 為了籌款他向行多有辈人拉關係
貿易商展 (尤指廚房)工作台 烤架

M : Welcome back from the trade fair, Michelle. Did you get any orders for our countertop grills?

W : I met a lot of new customers at the show, but I have so many business cards to sort out. It always takes so long. 我有好多卡片要整理 分類整理

application n. 應用程式, 申請者

M : You should download an app for your phone to organize them. I just found one called Digital Rolodex. You take a picture of each card and the app converts all the text to digital format. Then you can easily search for what you need. 名片/盒 v.轉換, 轉變 內文 數位形式

W : I could really use that. Is it free? 我真的用得上它 免費的嗎?

M : There is a free version, but the premium version lets you store an unlimited number of cards. It's well worth the price. 免費的版本 高級的, 優質的 無限數量的卡片

lead-led-led

56. (B) What has the woman recently done?
 (A) Led a product demonstration. 帶領(主持)一個產品展示
 (B) Attended a trade show. 參加貿易展
 (C) Ordered business cards. 整理過的卡片
 (D) Submitted a proposal. 提案

order v.命令, 訂購, 整理, 布置

57. (D) What does the man think the woman should do?
 (A) Write a review. 寫評論
 (B) Buy a new camera. 買新相機
 (C) Organize a party. 組織一個party
 (D) Use a phone application. app

58. (C) What does the man like about the premium version of a product?
 (A) It is easier to use. 方便使用
 (B) It is the industry standard. 業界標準, 工業標準
 (C) It has more storage space. 更收藏空間
 (D) It comes with warranty. 和保證書一起來

★warranty n. 保證書
under warranty
保固期內

Questions 59 through 61 refer to the following conversation.
補語

M : So, Ms. Binghampton, you believe that your lower back pain may be causing your headaches?

W : Well, I sit at a desk for 10 hours a day. 我一天坐在桌子前10小時

GO ON TO THE NEXT PAGE

M : I suggest you get up and stretch every 30 minutes when seated for long periods of time. Take a five-minute stroll around the office. Just something to get your blood moving.

W : Do I need to see a chiropractor about the back pain? 脊骨神經醫師

M : Not right now. Let's try this first. If the headaches continue, we'll consider seeing a specialist. 我們會考慮看專家(專科醫師)

chiropractic 脊骨按摩治療
practice 實行
* stretch 伸展
*stroll 散步

59. (C) Who most likely is the man?
(A) A mechanic. 機械工, 修理工
(B) A lawyer.
(C) A doctor.
(D) A teacher.

60. (D) Why does the woman say, "I sit at a desk for 10 hours a day"?
(A) To request a second opinion. 支他人的意見
(B) To apologize for an error. 為一個錯誤道歉
(C) To describe her area of expertise. 描述她的專業領域 (知識, 技術)
(D) To explain the cause of a problem. 解釋一個問題發生的原因

61. (D) What does the man recommend the woman do? 建議
(A) Rearrange her work space. 重新整理, 布置他的工作區
(B) Put her name on a waiting list. 把名字放在等待名單
(C) Join a fitness center.
(D) Take breaks at certain intervals. n. 間隔, 距離 at regular intervals 每隔定的 weekly 每隔一週
固定的間隔休息下

Questions 62 through 64 *refer to the following conversation and brochure.*
information technology — 內部的

M : I just heard at the staff meeting that our IT department manager, Mr. Edwards, is relocating out of state. I think they'll want someone internal to take over. 接管 + the mantle of sb. relocate v. 搬遷

W : I know. I'd be interested in being the next manager, but I'm a little nervous about applying. What if the hiring committee thinks I don't have a strong enough background in website administration? 假如雇用委員會覺得我沒有足夠的網站管理背景怎麼辦?

M : Well, the local community center offers advanced computer classes. You should enroll in one. 報名
當地的社區中心提供進階電腦課程

W : That'd be great if there's one I could attend. I work from 8 a.m. to 6 p.m. weekdays. So, 但願 hopefully, there's a session in the evening or on the weekend.

M : They offer different sessions, so I'm sure you'd find one that fits your schedule. 符合你的行程

員工會議宣布什麼?
62. (B) What was announced at the staff meeting?
(A) A sales event will be held. 銷售活動將被舉行
(B) An employee will leave the company.
(C) A merger will take place. 有個合併會發生
(D) A new product will be launched. 新產品會推出(上市)

56

63. (A) What is the woman nervous about doing? 她說緊張什麼事?
   (A) Applying for a job. 申請工作
   (B) Taking an exam. 參加考試
   (C) Being interviewed for an article. 因為一篇文章要訪
   (D) Starting her own company. 開始自己的公司

*餐廳相關英文
· I'd like to make a reservation.
Table for 2, please.

64. (D) Look at the graphic. Which session will the woman most likely attend?
   (A) Session 1. 資料庫管理
   (B) Session 2. 網路安全
   (C) Session 3. 網頁管理
   (D) Session 4. 〃

· Are you ready to order?
We need another minute.
· Check, please!
May I have the bill, please?

Radcliff Heights Community Center

· Would you like me to wrap this up?
wrap things up 打包

Advanced Computer Classes		
Session 1	Database Management	Mondays at 11:00 a.m.
Session 2	Network Security	Wednesdays at 5:30 p.m.
Session 3	Website Administration	Thursdays at 6:00 p.m.
Session 4	Website Administration	Saturdays at 1:00 p.m.

週末有空可以上課

Questions 65 through 67 refer to the following conversation and menu.

由於、因為、既然、

W : I hope you enjoyed your fish and chips. Can I bring you anything for dessert? It's included since you ordered the daily special. 由於你點了今日特餐、配包含甜點 一杯黑咖啡即可

M : The fish and chips were delicious, thanks, but I don't want any dessert. Just a cup of coffee, black, please. But I do have a question, though. Does your restaurant do any catering?

但我仍然有個問題 *though 放句尾:仍然、還是 你們餐廳有任何外燴服務嗎

W : Oh, certainly. I'll bring you our catering and takeout menu. Anything other than coffee I can get you? 當然. 提及 除了

M : Just the check, please. And I should mention that I have a coupon for 25 percent off my meal, so I'll be using that.

有效 一般餐點

W : I'm sorry, but unfortunately, that coupon is valid for regular menu items only, not the daily specials.

65. (B) Look at the graphic. What day is the conversation taking place?
   (A) Tuesday. *① 圖表.活動哪天舉行?
   (B) Wednesday.
   (C) Thursday. ② adj: 主動的、熱賣的
   (D) Friday.

GO ON TO THE NEXT PAGE

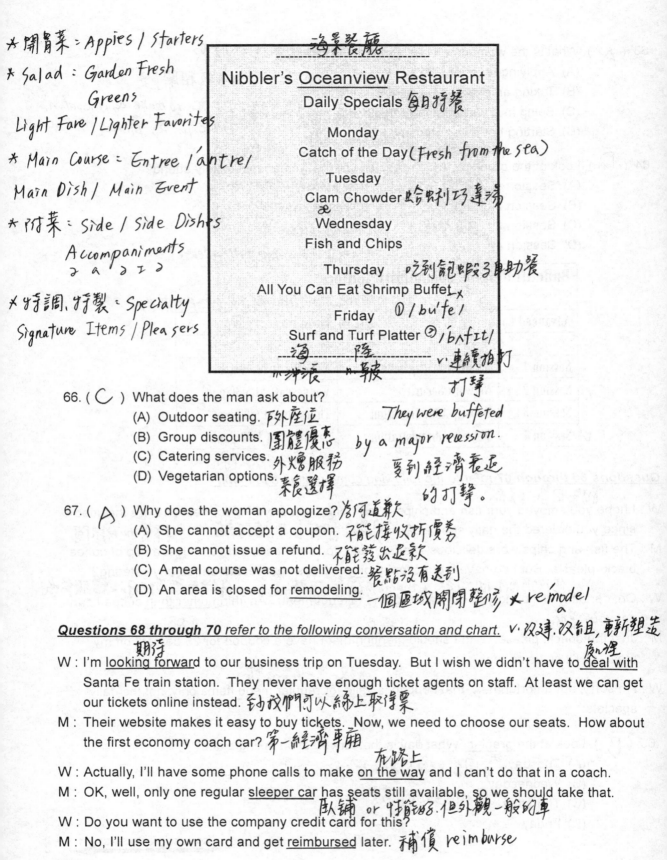

*開胃菜 = Appies / Starters

*Salad = Garden Fresh Greens

Light Fare / Lighter Favorites

*Main Course = Entree /ˈäntre/

Main Dish / Main Event

*附菜 = Side / Side Dishes

Accompaniments /ə a ə ɪ ə/

✗特調,特製 = Specialty

Signature Items / Pleasers

海景餐廳

Nibbler's Oceanview Restaurant

Daily Specials 每日特餐

Monday
Catch of the Day (Fresh from the sea)

Tuesday
Clam Chowder 蛤蜊巧達湯

Wednesday
Fish and Chips

Thursday
All You Can Eat Shrimp Buffet 吃到飽蝦子自助餐

Friday ① /buˈfe/
Surf and Turf Platter ② /bʌfɪt/

海 n·沙浪 ── 陸 n·軍隊 ── v·連續拍打 打擊

---

66. (C) What does the man ask about?
　　(A) Outdoor seating. 戶外座位
　　(B) Group discounts. 團體優惠
　　(C) Catering services. 外燴服務
　　(D) Vegetarian options. 素食選擇

They were buffeted by a major recession.
受到經濟衰退的打擊。

67. (A) Why does the woman apologize? 為何道歉
　　(A) She cannot accept a coupon. 不能接收折價券
　　(B) She cannot issue a refund. 不能發出退款
　　(C) A meal course was not delivered. 餐點沒有送到
　　(D) An area is closed for remodeling. 一個區域關閉整修 ✗ remodel

Questions 68 through 70 _refer to the following conversation and chart._ v·改建,改組,重新塑造
期待　　　　　　　　　　　　　　　　　　　　　　　　　　　　　處理

W : I'm looking forward to our business trip on Tuesday. But I wish we didn't have to deal with
　　Santa Fe train station. They never have enough ticket agents on staff. At least we can get
　　our tickets online instead. 動 我們可以線上取得票

M : Their website makes it easy to buy tickets. Now, we need to choose our seats. How about
　　the first economy coach car? 第一經濟車廂
　　　　　　　　　　　　　　　　　　在路上

W : Actually, I'll have some phone calls to make on the way and I can't do that in a coach.

M : OK, well, only one regular sleeper car has seats still available, so we should take that.
　　　　　　　　　臥鋪 or 特殊功能,但外觀一般的車

W : Do you want to use the company credit card for this?

M : No, I'll use my own card and get reimbursed later. 補償 reimburse

68. (C) Why does the woman dislike Santa Fe train station?
    (A) It has no Internet access. 不能上網 ＇access n.接近．進入
    (B) It is being renovated. 重整修
    (C) It is always understaffed. 總是人手不足
    (D) It is inconveniently located. 位子很不方便

69. (D) Look at the graphic. Which car will the speakers most likely choose?
    (A) Car 1.　　　✕ 兒童餐 Kids Menu
    (B) Car 2.　　　Juniors / Kids Stuff / For the Munchkins
    (C) Car 3.　　　Little Tikes (英)野狗．鄉巴佬．頑童) (小孩,無事忙的人)
    (D) Car 4.　　　／ɑɪ／

✕ 點餐相關補
充承博上題.

✕ 點心 Dessert
Sweets / Treats
For the sweet tooth.

✕ 飲料 Beverage
Refreshments. Drinks

✕ 酒類: Wine and Beer
Coolers, Draft
Liquor, From the Bar

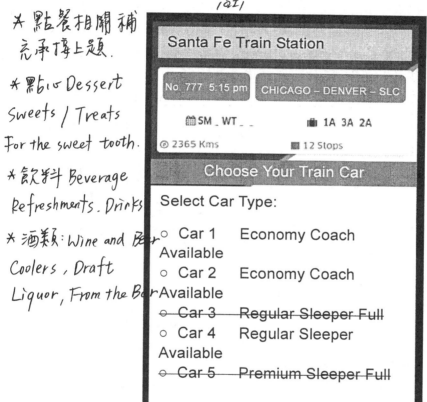

Santa Fe Train Station

No. 777 5:15 pm   CHICAGO – DENVER – SLC

SM _ WT _ _   1A 3A 2A

2365 Kms   12 Stops

Choose Your Train Car

Select Car Type:

○ Car 1   Economy Coach Available
○ Car 2   Economy Coach Available
○ Car 3   Regular Sleeper Full
○ Car 4   Regular Sleeper Available
○ Car 5   Premium Sleeper Full

70. (C) What does the woman ask the man about?
    (A) What time he wants to return. 何時想要回來
    (B) Where he wants to meet. 想要哪裡見面
    (C) How he wants to pay. 想如何付錢
    (D) How much luggage he is bringing. 帶多少行李

GO ON TO THE NEXT PAGE.

PART 4

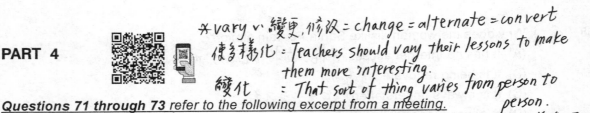

Questions 71 through 73 *refer to the following excerpt from a meeting.*

Obviously, we hold these manager meetings to secure and promote a consistent level of student satisfaction throughout our chain of language institutes. However, we've discovered that the quality of student experience varies from one location to the next. That's why I've hired Ms. Paulson here to develop monthly training sessions for full-time teachers at all of our locations. Managers, you'll be responsible for directing these sessions at each of your institutes. Only full-time teachers will be required to attend. Ms. Paulson is going to give you an overview of the sessions now. Let's welcome her.

71. (A) What industry do the managers work in?
    (A) Education.
    (B) Marketing.
    (C) Transportation.
    (D) Restaurant.

72. (C) According to the speaker, what area of the business needs to be improved?
    (A) Personnel retention.
    (B) Staff recruitment.
    (C) Customer service.
    (D) Curriculum preparation.

73. (D) What will the managers most likely do next?
    (A) Meet new students.
    (B) Submit student grade reports.
    (C) Conduct a training session.
    (D) Listen to a presentation.

Questions 74 through 76 *refer to the following telephone message.*

Hi, this is Charlotte Denier calling from Hacienda Hotel Group regarding your job application for the senior marketing position. Your resume is solid and we'd like to discuss this opportunity with you in person. But before we take the next step, I just want to remind you that the HHG marketing department has only recently been

60

developed and is still in the development stage. Thus, your initial duties may vary from time to time until we are fully staffed. If this is something you're interested in, give me a call back to set up a time for an interview. My number is 875-2233. Have a nice day.

仍然是在發展階段(未完成)。因此 你起初的責任可能因時間不同而有所不同，直到我們人員完全配置

74. (C) What type of company does the speaker work for?
    (A) An electronics manufacturer. 電子產品製造商
    (B) A travel agency. 旅遊公司
    (C) A hotel chain. 連鎖飯店
    (D) An accounting firm. 會計公司

* certificate
n. 證明書, 單據
certification
n. 證明, 檢定

75. (B) What does the speaker mention about the position? —提及
    (A) It requires official certification. 需要官方證明
    (B) It is in a newly established department. 新成立的部門
    (C) It involves frequent travel. 有參與時常旅行
    (D) It is a part-time position. 兼職職位

* confirm
v. 證實, 加強, 批准
→ The queen confirmed the treaty.
→ The latest developments confirmed me in my belief.

76. (C) Why is the listener asked to return a call?
    (A) To provide a reference. 提供佐證
    (B) To negotiate a salary. 討論薪水
    (C) To schedule an interview. 安排面試
    (D) To confirm a delivery. 確認貨運

Questions 77 through 79 *refer to the following excerpt from a meeting.*

OK, I think that just about covers everything for this marketing meeting. Oh, one more item. I want to take a minute to tell you about our new line of women's accessories, but we'll have to schedule a separate session for that next week. Meanwhile, I'd like you to take a look at the specifications of the new fall fashion line. The catalog can be found on the company website. Please be prepared to share your advertising strategy ideas for these products at our next meeting.

行銷會議
還有一件事
花一分鐘
全新系列的女性飾品
安排 不同的場部 同時
看看 細節, 規格
目錄 廣告
策略 想法

* specification
n. 載明, 詳述, 規格, 明細單
* specify v. 具體指定
詳細指明

77. (D) What department do the listeners work in?
    (A) Maintenance. 維護
    (B) Purchasing. 採購
    (C) Information Technology. 資訊科技
    (D) Marketing. 行銷

GO ON TO THE NEXT PAGE

78. (B) What does the speaker say is available on a company website?

(A) An employee directory. 通訊錄

(B) A catalog. 目錄 ≠ index 索引

(C) A map. 地圖

(D) A schedule. 行程

在公司網站上可以看到什麼

79. (C) What does the speaker ask the listeners to do at the next meeting?

(A) Choose a logo.

(B) Elect a representative. 選出一個代表人員

(C) Discuss their ideas.

(D) Sign a document. 簽文件

elect v. 選舉   adj. 卓越的, 當選的

n. 當選人, 被選定的人

Questions 80 through 82 refer to the following telephone message.

回電, 關於明天在你公司的演講

Good afternoon, Darren. This is Olivia returning your call about the presentation I'll be giving at your company tomorrow. You asked if I need any special equipment or materials. I'm actually bringing all the materials with me. Equipment-wise, the only thing I'll really need is a video projector screen. Oh, and about your suggestion to pick me up from the airport, I already hired a limousine service, but thank you for the consideration nevertheless. See you tomorrow!

特殊器材, 設備
材料
所有設備我都會自己帶
聰明的使用(引備(不需太多)
投影機   屏幕(下)
adv. 不過, 仍然

80. (D) What is the speaker preparing to do?

(A) Conduct a tour. 帶團, 帶參觀

(B) Organize a banquet. /bæŋkwɪt/ 宴會

(C) Travel overseas. 海外旅遊

(D) Give a presentation.

大轎車   ＊consideration
n. 考慮, 貼心, 關心, 重要

→ Cost is no consideration
費用不要緊

＊conduct
v. 引導, 實施, 處理

81. (D) What does the speaker request?

(A) A copy of a contract. 合約複本

(B) Access to a network.

(C) A list of guests. 賓客名單

(D) A video screen.

＊wise
adj. 有智慧的
明智的

82. (A) Why does the speaker say, "I already hired a limousine service"?

(A) To decline an offer. decline 婉拒, 下降, 衰落

(B) To explain a procedure. 流程

(C) To request directions.

(D) To propose a schedule change.

v. 提議, 建議, 提出

As one grows older
one's memory declines.

62

Here at Ridgemont Landscaping, we take safety very seriously, which is why we're holding this meeting today. Earlier this week, one of our installation sites was cited for multiple safety violations during a routine inspection. That is unacceptable. Let's begin by reviewing company safety policies. The binders on the table in front of you are yours to keep. They contain all our safety practices and they're divided into categories for your convenience. Unfortunately, I was pressed for time to get the materials together. I just noticed that some of the sections are out of order.

83. (B) What kind of business do the listeners most likely work for?
  (A) A shoe manufacturer.
  (B) A landscaping firm.
  (C) A utility company.
  (D) A food and beverage distributor.

84. (D) What is the purpose of the meeting?
  (A) To learn how to operate new equipment.
  (B) To discuss job openings.
  (C) To improve customer relations.
  (D) To review safety procedures.

85. (B) Why does the man say, "I was pressed for time to get the materials together"?
  (A) To praise an employee.
  (B) To provide an excuse.
  (C) To accept an apology.
  (D) To change a deadline.

Hi, this message is for Dylan Pietsch. My name is Susan and I'm one of the organizers of the Summer Music Festival. You recently sent us a registration form to reserve a booth at the fairgrounds. The problem is that it looks like you forgot to enclose the registration fee when you sent us the form. The fee is $250 per day and in order to be able to reserve a space for your company, we'll need the payment by next Friday. We're looking forward to having you there. It's going to be the biggest festival yet. Thousands of attendees have already registered and we're expecting many more to show up.

Please call me back if you have any questions. Thanks.

GO ON TO THE NEXT PAGE.

86. (D) What kind of event is the speaker organizing? ＊ yet
    (A) A fund-raising marathon. 募款馬拉松
    (B) An annual company outing. 年度公司旅遊 否定 They haven't met him yet.
    (C) A building dedication. 建物揭幕儀式 疑問 Have you finished yet?
    (D) A music festival. 音樂會
                                        總有一天 He will sutter for fun yet.
87. (D) What is the speaker's reason for calling? 再 I have yet another
討論活動 (A) To explain a recent change in policy.   question to ask.
內容 (B) To confirm the number of attendees.
content (C) To discuss the content of a performance. 而 My room is small yet cosy.
n.內容 (D) To request a missing payment. 缺少的款項
                                        還 There is hope for her yet.
88. (D) What does the speaker say about the event? 比較級專用 (更.益)
入場費增加(A) The admission fee has increased.   That job is yet more demanding.
    (B) There is limited seating. 位子有限
    (C) It will be held at a different location.
    (D) It will be well-attended. 出席人數很多

Questions 89 through 91 refer to the following announcement.

兩間公司的合併這個月會有定案
Thanks for being here this morning. As you know, the merger between Shipley
Industries and DBK Supply was finalized this month. As a result of our companies
由於公司人力加入
力力   自然會有組織改組
joining forces, there's naturally going to be some restructuring of the organization,
                                        新的工業設備部門頭頭
so I'm happy to announce that Norman Lee will be the new head of our industrial
部門   很開心他能擔任這個角色因為他是   cont.因為
equipment division. We're very excited that he's taking on this role since he's an
下 一個有能力的電氣工程師 上
accomplished electrical engineer. His experience will be an asset in this position.
Now, Norman is currently touring our factory in Oklahoma, but we expect him back
here next Tuesday. 參觀
                    發生
                    take place   他的經驗會是他職位的資產
89. (C) According to the speaker, what took place this month? (對他的工作加分)
    (A) A department training. 部門訓練
    (B) A product launch. 產品發表   ＊ accomplished
    (C) A company merger. 公司合併   adj. 熟練的, 有造詣的
    (D) A budget review. 預算審查   有教養的 an accomplished lady

90. (A) What is Norman Lee's field of expertise?
    (A) Electrical engineering.   ＊ —eer 人
    (B) Graphic design. 平面設計   mountaineer 登山者
    (C) Organic chemistry. 有機化學   pioneer 拓荒者
    (D) International law.   profiteer 奸商

64

91. (B) What is Norman Lee currently doing?
    (A) Developing a project budget. 做一個案子預算
    (B) Visiting a factory. 參觀工廠
    (C) Conducting an experiment. 做實驗
    (D) Meeting with the board of directors. 和董事會見面

experiment
Some people learn by experiment and others learn by experience.

Questions 92 through 94 *refer to the following instructions.*

Welcome to our first Hatha yoga class here at the Shiva Wellness Center. I'm your instructor, Ines. To start, let me point out those lockers at the back of the room. You can use them to store your mats and workout attire for the entire course. Also, I know the classes are listed on the program as being from 11 a.m. to 1 p.m. However, we'll end 10 minutes early, so we'll have time to put the room back together. We share this space with a meditation class. Oh, and one more thing. Before you leave tonight, don't forget to stop by the registration desk to pay for the class if you haven't done so already.

92. (D) What class does the speaker teach?
    (A) Graphic design. 平面設計
    (B) Computer programming. 設計電腦程式
    (C) Martial arts. 武術
    (D) Yoga. 瑜珈

register 註冊 = join
sign up 註冊
sign in 登入 sign out 登出
log in   log out

93. (C) Why does the speaker say, "We share this room with a meditation class"?
    (A) To invite students to another class. 邀請學生到另堂課
    (B) To remind participants to watch their belongings. 提醒參與者看顧好他們的東西
    (C) To stress the importance of finishing on time. 強調準時完成的重要性
    (D) To apologize for an inconvenient location. 道歉

94. (B) What are the listeners reminded to do before they leave? 他們離開之前被提醒做什麼?
    (A) Replace their desks. 桌子放回原處
    (B) Pay for registration. 付註冊費
    (C) Take some handouts. 拿一些講義，傳單，捐贈物
    (D) Provide some feedback. 提供些回饋

to rely on handouts 靠別人的施捨生活

GO ON TO THE NEXT PAGE.

Now for your KPRT local weather report. A storm passed through our city this morning, bringing much needed rain. Due to damage caused by the heavy winds earlier today, the traffic lights at the corner of Canfield Street and Swanson Avenue are not working. The traffic signals have been down for about an hour now and road crews have just started arriving to repair them. Officials report that the repairs should be finished by 6:00 p.m. and will not have any impact on tomorrow's 5K Run for Charity along Derby Street, so don't change your plans. We'll have more details about the race at the top of the hour.

95. (B) What caused a problem?
  (A) Building demolition.
  (B) Bad weather.
  (C) A train delay.
  (D) An auto accident.

96. (A) Look at the graphic. Which location is the speaker describing?
  (A) Location 1.
  (B) Location 2.
  (C) Location 3.
  (D) Location 4.

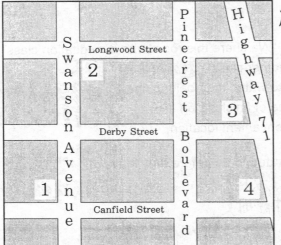

97. (B) What does the speaker say will take place tomorrow?
  (A) A grand opening.
  (B) A race.
  (C) A parade.
  (D) A musical performance.

Before we open the store today, let's go over our procedures for receiving book shipments. I'm concerned because a lot of time is wasted when these steps aren't followed. For example, sometimes cartons of books shipped from the company's warehouse are delivered to the wrong store. We don't want staff spending time inspecting merchandise that isn't meant for our store. So please pay attention to the store number the warehouse marks on each box. It must be the same as the number on the shipping invoice that's printed out daily. If not, we simply return the box unopened. It's important to remember this as we receive extra merchandise in preparation for the holiday season.

98. (A) What does the speaker say he is concerned about?
   (A) Wasted staff time.
   (B) Customer complaints.
   (C) Excessive absences.
   (D) Limited storage space.

99. (A) Look at the graphic. Which step does the speaker say requires special attention?
   (A) Step 1.
   (B) Step 2.
   (C) Step 3.
   (D) Step 4.

```
              Checklist
  1  _____
     Check store number
  2  _____
     Match titles with invoice
  3  _____
     Inspect books for damage
  4  _____
     Move items to storeroom
```

100. (D) What does the speaker say is going to happen?
   (A) A sales event will begin.
   (B) A branch store will close.
   (C) Fewer shipments will be sent out.
   (D) More merchandise will arrive.

GO ON TO THE NEXT PAGE.

READING TEST

*instruct → instruction n. → instructor n. 教師.講師 教練
v.指示.命令.指導 My job is to instruct her in English.

In the Reading test, you will read a variety of texts and answer several different types of reading comprehension questions. The entire Reading test will last 75 minutes. There are three parts, and directions are given for each part. You are encouraged to answer as many questions as possible within the time allowed.

You must mark your answers on the separate answer sheet. Do not write your answers in your test book.

*finance 'finance + pages 財經版
n.財政.金融 n.資金.財政 + minister 財務長
v.提供資金.融資 Our project is adequately financed.

PART 5

Directions: A word or phrase is missing in each of the sentences below. Four answer choices are given below each sentence. Select the best answer to complete the sentence. Then mark the letter (A), (B), (C), or (D) on your answer sheet.

超過10年前, Dean 離開了1個很有前途的職業
在金融領域裡的.加入了間草創公司.

所有旅遊相關的業務支出(花費)
應該要繳交給會計部門

101. More than a decade ago, Dean Lorber ------- a promising career in finance to join a start-up company.
(A) will leave
(B) was left
(C) leave
(D) left
[D] left (up)

102. On-going road construction on southbound Route 83 has ------- traffic delays at the Carlton Interchange.
(A) directed 指揮 ≠ intersection + 字路口
(B) operated operate 運作.營業
(C) caused cause 引起
(D) instructed
[C] caused (up)
正在進行的.繼續的 道路建設
交流道

103. Mr. Wanshack requests that the research team e-mail the final report to ------- before 5:30 p.m.
(A) his
(B) himself
(C) him
(D) he
[C] him
v. (O)

I	me		we	us
you	you		you	you
he	him		they	them
she	her			
it	it			

104. Geartex ------- sends e-mails with discount codes to customers who have registered for premium accounts.
(A) nearly 幾乎.差不多
(B) often
(C) highly 高度地
(D) ever 從未.至今
[B]
often
寄送有
折扣碼的
信件給優質客戶
→He is highly premium paid. adj.高價的
薪水很高 優質的

105. All travel-related business expenses should be ------- to the accounting department.
(A) submitted
(B) submissions
(C) submit
(D) submits
[A]
*technical adj.工藝的.技術的
專門的.技術上更高提高
→Technical advances improve productivity

106. Customers should contact the manufacturer ------- for any technical support.
(A) direct
(B) directing
(C) directly
(D) direction
[C]
directly
有任何技術/專業上的需求
都該直接向製造商
聯絡。

107. Passengers must show both boarding passes and passports ------- boarding the plane.
(A) how
(B) when
(C) as
(D) if
[B]
when
當登機時.登機證和護照都要拿出來
*morale n.士氣.鬥志.道德
(A) 8 x
(B) reality n.現實 x
(C) closure 結束.關閉
(D) consequence n.結果.後果

108. One of the major challenges companies must deal with is maintaining employee morale.
(A) morale
(B) reality
(C) closure
(D) consequence
[A]
公司要處理的重要挑戰之一
就是如何維持員工士氣。
重要性
He is a man of great consequence. 是個重要人物。

14

109. Seminar attendees at the Civic Center are reminded that roads in the vicinity are ------- crowded during peak hours.
(A) usually
(B) exactly
(C) finely
(D) cleanly

(handwritten) 公民中心參加研討會的人被提醒 尖峰時刻附近區域的交通擁擠 精細地: These instruments are finely set. 這些樂器是精細調過的 阿附近區域

110. During ------- his period of unemployment, Dylan applied to over a dozen law firms.
(A) Between
(B) During
(C) Behind
(D) From

(handwritten) 在他沒工作的期間，他申請了 超過10幾間法務公司 * a long dozen 13個 (B) 有競爭力的，好競爭的

111. Omega Airlines is expanding its regional flight coverage to maintain a ------- edge in the transportation marketplace.
(A) competition
(B) competitive
(C) competitively
(D) compete

(handwritten) OA在拓展它的區域班機涵蓋範圍，去維持它在運輸市場上的競爭優勢。優勢 交通車輛市

112. Ms. Mathers laid out the marketing campaign before ------- sales figures prior to the campaign's launch.
(A) cooperating
(B) designing
(C) purchasing
(D) announcing

(handwritten) lay out ①展開 ②展示 ③用錢 ④計劃 cooperate 合作 design 設計 purchase 購買 announce 宣佈 專案經理的責任 銷售數據 之前

113. It is the project manager's responsibility to make sure that all custom products meet the client(s) -------.
(A) specific
(B) to specify
(C) specifically
(D) specifications

(handwritten) 客製化商品 +N. 特殊的，明確的，具體的 指定，明確說明 The directions specify how the medicine is to be used. 規格，詳述

114. Passengers are reminded to stow their ------- baggage in the overhead compartments.
(A) unlimited
(B) personal
(C) accurate
(D) temporary

(handwritten) 所有格 +N. 收 無限的 個人的 正確的 暫時的 旅客被提醒把個人的東西收在頭頂上的置物箱 * compartment ①隔間: The dresser drawer was partitioned into four compartments. ②火車上小客房

115. A merger of the two companies is one ------- outcome of the meeting between the two CEOs.
(A) possibilities
(B) possibly
(C) possible
(D) possibility

(handwritten) 合併 兩公司的合併是2個CEO會面的結果可能 possibly adv. possible adj.+N 可能的 N.可能的人選 possibility n.可能性 She sounds like a possible.

116. Please ------- all sections of the lease application and provide a signature where indicated.
(A) mature
(B) deliver
(C) terminate
(D) complete

(handwritten) 租約 申請表 mature adj. 成熟的 ⇄ amateur adj. 外行的 terminate v. 終止 complete v. 完成 並在指示的地方 簽署

117. At Concordia, the ------- has always been on building customer relationships, not on increasing profits.
(A) emphasis
(B) emphasize
(C) emphasized
(D) emphatic

(handwritten) +N. 總是強調建立客戶關係 而不是增加利潤 emphasis n. emphasize v. emphasized v. an emphatic < refusal denial emphatic adj. 堅決的，強調的

118. ------- presenting a valid photo ID, customers may claim parcels from Allied Air Express.
(A) Upon
(B) Among
(C) Without
(D) Over

(handwritten) 怎領取包裹 Upon 在~一旦/在~以後/根據 Among 在~之中 Without 沒有 Over 在~正上方 adj. 高聳的，激烈的: He was in a towering rage. 很生氣

119. At a towering height of 1,400 feet, Willis Tower can be seen from ------- in the metropolitan area.
(A) absolutely
(B) around
(C) entirely
(D) anywhere

(handwritten) 在都市區的任何地方 absolutely 絕對地 around adv. Please drive me around. entirely 完全地 That's entirely up to you. ①N.任何地方 ②接肯定句 adv.

120. Mr. Jenkins suggests that we ------- the shipment until the order is complete.
(A) delay
(B) expire
(C) wait
(D) remain

(handwritten) Did you go anywhere last night? You can't get it anywhere.

GO ON TO THE NEXT PAGE.

121. All department supervisors are encouraged to familiarize ------- with the minimum standards required for occupational safety. 職業安全

熟悉

(A) they 句子中的 S.和 O.為同一人時,用反身代N.
(B) theirs　myself　himself　ourselves　themselves
(C) their　yourself　herself　yourselves
✓ (D) themselves

答 D

任何和這個月任務(工作)相關的問題

122. Any questions ------- this month's assignments should be directed to Mr. Shaffer. 應該提交給 shaffer 先生

conj. 因為/雖然

(A) up on
(B) according to 根據
(C) related to 相關
(D) through 徹底地.完全地

答 C

盡管/當…時/像
The work is not so difficult as you imagine.

As the sun rose the fog dispersed. 霧散開 /tenjur/ n. 任期

10801

123. At the current rates of production, Astra Industries will manufacture enough products to meet expected demand by this summer. 以目前的生產率而言.AI會在這個夏天

(A) find 之前 生產足夠 符合需求量的商品
(B) meet
(C) enroll
(D) contact ✗ rumor
v. 謠傳 n. 謠言

meet

Company corporation

答 B

124. Roster Industries and Charleston Co. are rumored to be close to completing their merger.

close

(A) closeness N.
(B) closing
(C) closely
(D) close

接近片語 完成他們的合併 內部審查

答 D

從媒體中心拿出(借出)的器材一定要在

125. Equipment checked out from the media center must be returned within two weeks of the date it was borrowed.

within

(A) by 借出日期 2 週內歸還。
(B) within
(C) at 一開始. S 博士把實驗 結果歸因於
(D) before 不好的 機器,可是他最近用新設備
　　　　也遇到了相同的結果.

答 B

✗ faulty 有缺點的.不完美的

126. Jackson Innovations discontinued one of their products, The Stomper ------- due to safety concerns. JI 有項商品不再生產了,

(A) reporting (TS)
(B) reports 據說是由於安全考量.補充說
(C) reported 明的副
(D) reportedly 據傳聞.據報導 用adv.

答 D

127. The new Exgenera smart phone will not come out this month, ------- even next month, as the company is facing major design issues right now.

or

(A) whether 這個月不會出,或是甚至下個月
(B) by 也不會,因為公司正面臨重大的
(C) through 設計問題。(整個任期內)
(D) or

答 D

128. Throughout his tenure, Mr. Spears has shown a great ------- to our university for the last three decades. 過去 30 年來對學校

(A) collaboration 合作 很付出.很忠誠
(B) resignation 辭職.放棄.辭呈 resign v.
(C) assurance 保證.信心
(D) commitment 保證.信心
　　　　奉獻.承諾.承擔的義務

答 D

129. Disappointed with the results of an internal audit, the president of Slantron Ltd. ------- reorganized the accounting and compliance departments.

adv.

(A) prompt adj.
(B) promptly adv. He promptly forgot all about it.
(C) promptness n.
(D) prompter ↘ He replied with promptness and courtesy.

提詞人/機;激勵者

對於內部審查結果失望,S公司 董事長寫上重整會計和法令部門

內部審查

答 B

130. At first, Dr. Sampson ------- the result of his experiment to a faulty machine, but he recently had the same result with new equipment.

attribute to

(A) attributes 把~歸因於 象徵
(B) attributed attribute n. 屬性.特質
(C) attributing → Kindness is one of her
(D) attribution 　　 attributes.

仁慈是她的特質之一

答 B

Directions: Read the texts that follow. A word, phrase, or sentence is missing in parts of each text. Four answer choices are given below each of the texts. Select the best answer to complete the text. Then mark the letter (A), (B), (C), or (D) on your answer sheet.

Questions 131-134 refer to the following advertisement.

SPECIAL OFFER FROM OAKWOOD SPORTING GOODS

It's here—our end-of-season camping equipment sales event!
As a previous customer of Jericho Sporting Goods, you _____ 131.
for a special offer not available to the public. We are offering
25 percent off on all camping and outdoor _____ 132.

No down payment required! _____ 133. customers who apply for
in-house financing during this sales event can receive twelve
months of no-interest payments.

_____ 134. This offer expires December 15.

131. (A) qualifies
(B) to qualify
(C) qualify
(D) qualified

132. (A) gears
(B) geared
(C) gearing
(D) gear

133. (A) In addition
(B) As a result
(C) In contrast
(D) Even though

134. (A) A payment on your Oakwood Sporting Goods credit card is due
(B) Your account has recently been suspended
(C) We encourage you to visit us during the sales event
(D) Your first payment is due the end of November

Questions 135-138 refer to the following article.

PITTSBURGH — Shelton's Steak House, a new restaurant located in the Riverside neighborhood, will open for business on May 3. The restaurant will offer a meat-lovers menu that emphasizes ------- ingredients. Shelton's specializes in steaks from Certified Angus beef, and American Yorkshire pork chops, flame-grilled over mesquite charcoal. The restaurant will be open for lunch Monday through Sunday from 11 A.M. to 3 P.M. and for dinner from 5 P.M. until 10 P.M. -------. "Those looking for a great steak or chop are invited to stop by our restaurant." said owner Gordon Shelton. "We welcome the opportunity to ------- both area residents and tourists."

135. (A) will locate
(B) locates
(C) located
(D) is located

136. (A) used
(B) separate
(C) sweet
(D) quality

137. (A) The restaurant might reopen in a different part of town
(B) These hours are similar to those of nearby eateries
(C) Customers have already provided some online reviews
(D) The restaurant has a simple, deep sea decor

138. (A) thank
(B) serve
(C) visit
(D) preserve

18

To: staff@melvoinindustries.com

From: d_timmons@melvoinindustries.com

Date: June 22

Subject: Zero Waste box

I am ------- to announce that our office has enrolled in an E-Waste

139.

recycling program through a company called Zero Waste. You

may have already noticed the Zero cardboard box next to the

printer. -------. Zero Waste sent this box to us to collect our used

140.

and unwanted electronic gadgets. Once the box is -------, I will

141.

ship it to the Zero Waste recycling facility, and we will be sent a

new one. Be sure to put only electronic waste in the box. The

company does not accept other -------. Thank you all for helping

142.

in our efforts to keep harmful metals and chemicals out of our

landfills.

Best,

Dan Timmons

Office Manager, Melvoin Industries

139. (A) pleasing
(B) pleasure
(C) please
(D) pleased

140. (A) It arrived a few days ago
(B) Let me know if it still works
(C) Just press the power button
(D) Take as many as you like

141. (A) found
(B) broken
(C) full
(D) clean

142. (A) ideas
(B) materials
(C) payments
(D) visitors

GO ON TO THE NEXT PAGE

Questions 143-146 refer to the following letter.

*national n. nation n. 國家
adj. 全國性的 national newspapers ② n. 國民 Foreign nationals were
國有的 national railroad asked to leave the country.
*reliant adj. 依賴的
They are reliant on unemployment benefit.
靠失業救濟生活

October 3

Terry Blankenship
80 West 34th Avenue
Kansas City, MO 64899

Dear Mr. Blankenship,

On behalf of the National Karate Museum, I want to thank you
for your gift of $10,000. We are largely reliant on ------- like yours
143.
to maintain the quality of our exhibitions and related events. We
appreciate your willingness to help us continue to grow and to
make our museum ------- to as many people as possible.
144.
As one of our valued donors, you ------- to our Annual Supporters
145.
Gala later this year. ------- If you are in Colorado Springs at that
146.
time, we certainly hope to see you there.

Sincerely,

D. Q. Finley
Development Coordinator, National Karate Museum

143. (A) moments
(B) assistants
(C) contributions
(D) recommendations

144. (A) accessibly
(B) accessible
(C) accessed
(D) accessibility

145. (A) will be invited
(B) would have invited
(C) will invite
(D) would have been invited

146. (A) We have been in Colorado Springs for over twenty years
(B) Your keynote address was particularly inspiring
(C) The museum is open six days a week all year long
(D) More details about this event will be available soon

20

PART 7

Directions: In this part you will read a selection of texts, such as magazine and newspaper articles, e-mails, and instant messages. Each text or set of texts is followed by several questions. Select the best answer for each question and mark the letter (A), (B), (C), or (D) on your answer sheet.

Questions 147-148 refer to the following Web page.

http://www.patagonia.com

ECLIPSE

Download now!

ONLY $15.99

15 tracks — 70 minutes

ECLIPSE — Bradley Swann and the Hot Rocks

Award-winning singer-songwriter Bradley Swann opens a new chapter in his career as he releases *Eclipse*, his first live album and his first album with new backing band Hot Rocks and new label partners Westin Music Group. Recorded live during a week-long residency at the Condor Theater in Los Angeles, California, *Eclipse* features guest appearances from Luke Landy and Niles Plantangel. The DVD will also include special behind-the-scenes footage and content with Swann discussing the inspiration behind his return to live performance.

---

147. What is indicated about *Eclipse*?

(A) It was recorded during a series of live performances.
(B) It will be released next year.
(C) It is only available in one format.
(D) It consists entirely of new songs.

148. What is stated about Bradley Swann?

(A) He has played with musicians from different countries.
(B) He has won awards for his music.
(C) He retired from the music business nearly a decade ago.
(D) He lives in Memphis, Tennessee.

GO ON TO THE NEXT PAGE.

Questions 149-150 refer to the following form.

CITY OF BROOMFIELD
住戶回饋表格 **RESIDENT FEEDBACK FORM**

Name:	Ted Sippy	**Phone:**	(708)323-3459
Address:	9008 Belmont Avenue		
Neighborhood:	West Irving 請你細描述你關心/擔心的事和建議		

Please detail your concerns and/or suggestions below:

自從 HR 開始做工程之後
Ever since construction began on Historic Route 66 (State Rte. 180),
交通變得非常擁擠   在PP交流道的附近區域
traffic has been very congested in the vicinity of the Ponderosa
                                    I.C.3I.C 交通特別地不好
Parkway interchange (Interstate 40). Traffic is particularly bad
在尖峰時刻   因此,   很多駕駛試圖
during rush hours. As a result, many drivers are attempting to
繞道 繞過這個問題區域   藉由BA   BA
detour around this problem area by using Belmont Avenue, which
/ditur/   直接切過WI   WI是個住宅區
cuts through West Irving, a residential neighborhood. In my
(利用WI這件事)   /rɛzɪdɛnʃ(ə)l/ adj.居住的
opinion, this practice must stop. I urge the city to re-route vehicles
n.實施 練習   應該要停止 力勸   重新安排行車路線
without passing through our community. Only then can West
不要通過我們社區
Irving return to being the peaceful and safe area it once was.
只有到了那時(車子不通過我們社區),社區才會變回以往的和平安全區

*only放句首 only +adv. +助V. + S + V原
後面倒裝   +bev. +S
        填意

149. Why did Mr. Sippy fill out the form?
C (A) To support an upcoming 即將到來的
    construction project. 建設案
(B) To contest the removal of traffic
    signals. 交通號誌移除提出質疑
(C) To protest an increase in local
    traffic. 抗議當地交通增加
(D) To criticize a historic tour.
    批評一個有歷史意義的導覽,參觀 (看先展示意味類)

150. What is suggested about Belmont
A Avenue? 通常很安靜
(A) It was usually quiet. →穿越
(B) It crosses Ponderosa Parkway.
(C) It is under construction. 在做工程
(D) It has several fast-food restaurants
    along it. 沿著這條路有好幾間 速食餐廳

22

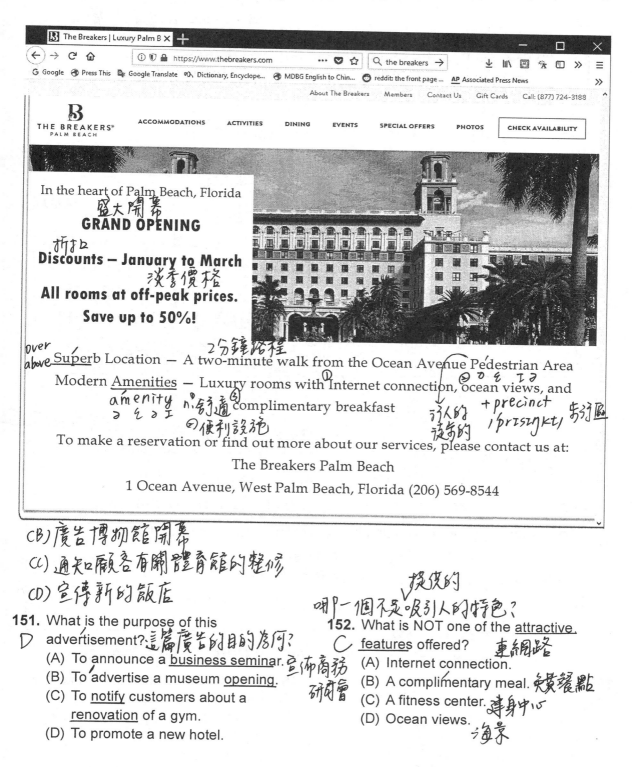

In the heart of Palm Beach, Florida

GRAND OPENING

Discounts – January to March

All rooms at off-peak prices.

Save up to 50%!

Superb Location — A two-minute walk from the Ocean Avenue Pedestrian Area

Modern Amenities — Luxury rooms with Internet connection, ocean views, and complimentary breakfast

To make a reservation or find out more about our services, please contact us at:

The Breakers Palm Beach

1 Ocean Avenue, West Palm Beach, Florida (206) 569-8544

151. What is the purpose of this advertisement?
(A) To announce a business seminar.
(B) To advertise a museum opening.
(C) To notify customers about a renovation of a gym.
(D) To promote a new hotel.

152. What is NOT one of the attractive features offered?
(A) Internet connection.
(B) A complimentary meal.
(C) A fitness center.
(D) Ocean views.

GO ON TO THE NEXT PAGE.

Questions 153-154 refer to the following memo.

internship n. 實習醫生的地位
paid internship 有薪實習

To: All Spectra Branding Supervisors and Design Interns
From: Jill Boursten, Office Manager
Date: Friday, October 5   *in-house 內部的*   *n. 實習醫生,師.*   *v. 拘留*
Subject: In-house software workshop   *軟體工作坊*

The in-house software workshop for new graphic design interns
scheduled for Monday, October 8, at 9:00 a.m. has been postponed.
This workshop is designed to familiarize interns with the software used
by the creative department to format and develop all Spectra branding
efforts. Mason Reeves, the senior creative associate who developed the software,
is unavailable on Monday. He has been asked to make an appearance
at the CORE Marketing Summit in New York on both Monday and
Tuesday. The workshop will therefore be rescheduled for Friday,
October 12, at 10:00 a.m. Interns who are unable to attend this session
are asked to notify their supervisors as soon as possible. Creative
department supervisors, please ensure that all interns within your
department are aware of the change by the end of the day today.

Thank you,
Jill

新的平面設計實習生
原訂安排在周一
已被延期
創意部門　*複*　*Spectrum (單) 光譜*
品牌建立的努力(成就)　*格式化, 編排*
這個工作坊是設計來讓實習生熟悉創意部用來編排和發展光譜品牌拓展的軟體
周一沒空　*資深的 創意部同事,夥伴,就是開發這個軟體的人*
他被要求要露臉
行銷高峰會上
重新安排到周五
實習生 不能參加這個活動的
複試要通知他們的長官　*信狀*
確保
意識到(知道)　*行程有改*

＊ familiarize with 使熟悉,親切
→ she tried to familiarize himself with the use of the new tool.
＊ effort 努力
→ It's not worth the effort to write. 不值得死努力去寫.

---

153. What is the memo about?
A
- (A) A schedule change. *行程改變*
- (B) A software update. *軟體更新*
- (C) A hiring policy. *雇用政策*
- (D) A company outing. *公司旅遊*

154. According to the memo, on what day will a workshop take place?
D
- (A) Monday. *工作坊哪天舉行?*
- (B) Tuesday.
- (C) Thursday.
- (D) Friday.

24

Questions 155-157 refer to the following e-mail.

From:	a.abdul@javaplanet.com
To:	gil.manning@houstonorganicherald.com
Re:	Jave Planet
Date:	July 27

📎 Java Beans Itinerary (2.67MB)

Dear Mr. Manning,

Everybody at Java Planet loves your popular website, which is an excellent resource for green-minded consumers in Houston. Since your site contains a list of related events in the area, I am writing to inform you of upcoming promotional activities for Earth Planet. I hope you will share this information with your readers.

Earth Planet has produced organic whole roasted coffee since our founding more than a decade ago, and we have just launched a unique blend of two exotic varieties from Sumatra and Bolivia. To advertise this line, Earth Planet will be distributing free samples at coffee shops, supermarkets, and health-food specialty outlets for the next few months. For your reference, I have attached the locations and dates of our marketing tour.

Should you have any questions or require additional information, feel free to contact me or visit our website, www.javaplanet.com. Furthermore, if you would like to try some of our products, please send your address, and I will be happy to oblige.

Sincerely,

Aliya Abdul
Vice President, Java Planet

---

155. What does Ms. Abdul ask Mr. Manning to do?
(A) Publicize some events.
(B) Attend a grand opening.
(C) Sponsor a marketing tour.
(D) Make an online donation.

156. What does Ms. Abdul offer to send?
(A) Order forms.
(B) Coffee samples.
(C) A press release.
(D) An offer of employment.

157. What is indicated about Java Planet?
(A) It recently opened a café in Houston.
(B) It owns a number of health-food stores.
(C) It has expanded its line of products.
(D) It will be launching a new website.

GO ON TO THE NEXT PAGE

★ StarTribune

BUSINESS

☽ 30° FORECAST | TRAFFIC

Weekly ads

Home | Local | Sports | Business | Opinion | Variety | Obituaries | Classifieds | Autos | Housing | Jobs

Lighthizer to Expand This Summer

(NEW HAVEN) – According to a statement issued on Monday, Lighthizer's Brewery, headquartered in New Haven, has purchased the former Stamford Lumber Warehouse in Bridgeport. The 172-year-old brewery had hinted earlier this year that it planned to extend its market into Long Island and New York. Renovations to the 30,000-square-meter site are expected to begin in July, with the plant ready for operations in December.

Lighthizer's began as a small family-owned brewery in New Haven. Over the years, it has grown and opened breweries throughout Connecticut, including two in Stamford and three in Hartford. Lighthizer's now earns revenues of more than 300 million each year and has become one of the largest breweries on the East Coast.

In the past, Lighthizer's produced mainly Pilsner and Lager style beers. It also developed a reputation for its unique Uncle Bill's Pale Ale. Recently, however, the company has branched out into the specialty market, producing a variety of hand-made craft brews. It is not yet known if the Bridgeport plant will produce any new products.

158. What is the purpose of the article?

(A) To support an upcoming business merger.

(B) To announce the completion of a renovation project.

(C) To review a new product line.

(D) To report on a company's expansion.

159. What new items have recently been added to Lighthizer's product line?

(A) Pilsners.

(B) Lagers.

(C) Pale Ales.

(D) Craft beers.

160. Which Lighthizer's Brewery location is currently NOT producing any products?

(A) New Haven.

(B) Bridgeport.

(C) Stamford.

(D) Hartford.

SANTA BARBARA WINE COUNTRY
Only an hour from L.A.!

Spring is the perfect time for a visit to Santa Barbara Wine Country. Escape the crowded city streets for some relaxation.

Below is a sampling of what Santa Barbara has to offer at this beautiful time of year.

Wine Tastings — Delight your palette with Santa Barbara's only Master Sommelier, Rene Duchance, head winemaker at Cortesa Valley Vineyards. For the spring season, Mr. Duchance has chosen an especially inviting theme: Twenty Vineyards, Twenty Varietals. Purchase your tickets now at cortesavalley.com/20-20.

Mission Tours — Enjoy the breathtaking views of Santa Barbara Lake from the area's most famous Spanish mission, San Pancho. Tours run Tuesday through Sunday starting in May. There is no charge for tours, but they must be booked in advance.

Horseback Rides — Take advantage of the rustic terrain with an adventurous horseback ride on Santa Barbara Trail. Fares increase in the summer, and so do the tourists, so book your ride for early in the season. Horseback rides are available several times every day.

Hiking and Biking — The Santa Barbara National Park's many hiking trails can accommodate hikers of all levels. New color-coded maps have been posted throughout the park for your convenience and bicycles are now permitted on certain paths! Before bicycling, be sure to read all guidelines for riding in the park, available on the Santa Barbara National Park page of our website.

Shakespeare on the Lawn — All plays are performed by local actors and theater students. Our season begins on April 7, with shows every Saturday and Sunday at 2:00 p.m. Children under five are free. Performances take place only if weather permits. Refunds are offered in case of inclement weather.

For more information, please go to: sbwinecountry.com

161. What is being advertised?
(A) Events to celebrate Santa Barbara's anniversary.
(B) Seasonal activities at a tourist destination.
(C) A contest to win a vacation package.
(D) Tours of a newly renovated area.

162. What is indicated about the plays?
(A) They are performed in April only.
(B) They are canceled when it rains.
(C) They feature famous actors.
(D) They receive excellent reviews.

163. According to the advertisement, why should people visit the Santa Barbara Wine Country page?
(A) To book a tour of San Pancho Mission.
(B) To rent a bicycle for riding on the park trails.
(C) To learn about the rules for biking in the park.
(D) To purchase tickets for guided tours of the park.

GO ON TO THE NEXT PAGE

27

MEMORANDUM

ATTENTION:

All Johnson University graduate students residing in Hyde Park Dormitory

Date: August 24

We have been informed that the West Kennedy exit on the Fuller Expressway will be closed for repairs during the month of September between 8:00 a.m. and 5:00 p.m., Mondays through Saturdays. West Kennedy traffic will be redirected to the Hyde Park exit. If you are accustomed to using the West Kennedy exit to travel to the Silverstein Conservatory, please leave for classes early so you can still arrive on campus on schedule.

In response to the inconvenience, Dr. Virgil has offered to take extra passengers in his minivan each day. If you are interested in carpooling, please contact him directly. Dr. Virgil can accommodate five passengers on a first-come-first-served basis and asks $3.00 per day as compensation.

164. What is the memo mainly about?
(A) A change in a school schedule.
(B) The relocation of a bus stop.
(C) The impact of road construction.
(D) An application to live in a dormitory.

165. What is indicated about Dr. Virgil?
(A) He lives in West Kennedy.
(B) He starts work at 8:00 a.m.
(C) He can take some students to the university.
(D) He works at a hospital.

166. What are students encouraged to do?
(A) Reschedule their classes.
(B) Use public transportation.
(C) Attend a staff meeting.
(D) Allow extra time for travel.

167. The word "compensation" in paragraph 2, line 4, is closest in meaning to
(A) fuel.
(B) payment.
(C) correction.
(D) selection.

FOR IMMEDIATE RELEASE
Charles to Deliver Keynote at Meet_QLoc

LAS VEGAS (January 10) – Holden D. Charles, President of DMZ Computer Services, will deliver the keynote address at the Meet_QLoc User's Group Meeting to be held on February 20 at 9:00 a.m. in the Fulbright Ballroom of the Starwood Hotel in Las Vegas, Nevada.

Charles's talk, entitled "Multimedia Databases," will focus on methods to integrate images, sounds, and videos into QLoc databases. The registration fee is $125 for the entire day and includes lunch. Pre-registration is required due to seating limitations.

DMZ specializes in providing database solutions using QLoc. For more information on Charles's talk, contact Jane Qunnepac at (202) 445-1230. To register for the meeting, call the Washington-area QLoc Users' Group at (202) 445-8899.

168. What is the main purpose of the press release?
(A) To announce a business seminar.
(B) To promote a new project.
(C) To clarify the details of a merger.
(D) To request feedback from the public.

169. What will Mr. Charles most likely do on February 20?
(A) Sign a contract.
(B) Give a speech.
(C) Travel overseas.
(D) Take a new position.

170. What is included in the $125 registration fee?
(A) Parking.
(B) Transportation.
(C) A meal.
(D) A souvenir.

171. What is stated about DMZ Technologies?
(A) They specialize in databases.
(B) They are hosting the seminar.
(C) They are merging with another company.
(D) They are seeking new investors.

GO ON TO THE NEXT PAGE

Florence Pineda 訂單寄出了嗎？如果還沒有， 10:25 AM
John, has order JP-7326 been sent out yet? If not, the customer
has asked us to add item JD-6455A. 客戶要求我們再加入商品JD-6455A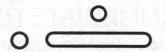

John D'Angelo 那是客製化的皮夾克對吧嗎 10:28 AM 刺繡
That's a <u>customized</u> <u>leather jacket</u>, right? The embroidery
department usually requires a minimum of three days to
<u>personalize</u> an item.　要求最少3個工作日來個人化一項商品

Florence Pineda 可以更快做好這商品嗎？ 10:29 AM
Can you get it any sooner? The customer needs it as soon as
possible. 客戶想盡快拿到

John D'Angelo 讓我來問問刺繡部的人 10:31 AM
Let me check with someone from embroidery.

John D'Angelo 可以幫我趕工嗎？ 10:33 AM
Dawn, can you do a rush job on a jacket? It's item JD-6455A
for order number JP-7326.

Dawn Foster 10:34 AM
How soon do you need it? Is tomorrow OK?

Florence Pineda 10:35 AM
Yes, <u>that will have to do</u>. Thank you both for your help!
=that will do 謝謝你倆的幫忙

那樣可以

172. What type of products does the store sell? 這問店賣什麼商品?
C
(A) Musical instruments. 音樂樂器
(B) Jewelry. /dʒuərI/ 珠寶
(C) Clothing. 衣服
(D) Appliances. 電器 (electrical appliance)

173. Why does Mr. D'Angelo contact Ms. Foster? 知道會議何時舉行
C
(A) To find out when a meeting will be held. 通知(告知)她之前訊息有個錯誤
(B) To alert her to an error in a previous message. 詢問有個工作是否可以比
(C) To ask if some work can be completed faster than usual. 一般狀況快點完成
(D) To find out when an order will be shipped. 知道何時送貨.

174. What does the customer want to do?
A
(A) Change an order. 改變訂單
(B) Update a delivery address. 更新貨運地址
(C) Receive a refund. 收退款
(D) Choose a different shipping method. 選個不同的方法運送

175. At 10:35, what does Ms. Pineda most likely mean when she writes, "that will have to do"?
B
(A) She plans to interview someone for a job. (否) 滿意
(B) She is satisfied with Ms. Foster's response. 回應 (下)
(C) The customer will be upset if the job can't be completed.
(D) Some new items will be chosen for a catalog by the end of the day.

(upset adj. 心煩的.苦腦的
→ 有些新商品會被送來
叙在目錄裡,今天下班3前

＊satisfy
①·滿意·滿足 (需要.欲望)
Our company will do everything to satisfy our customers

②達到 (要求.標準)
You can't apply for this job until you have satisfied certain conditions.

③履行　双方都努力履行這個合約
Both sides strove to satisfy the contract.
v. strive 奮鬥

④清除　他一席話清除了她的疑慮
His remarks satisfied her doubts.

⑤使確信　你能否確信他在說真話呢?
Are you satisfied that he is telling the truth?

GO ON TO THE NEXT PAGE.

*look through   識破敵人的詭計

1. 識破: We have looked through the enemy's tricks.
2. 瀏覽

From the desk of

RICHARD & LOIS WEBBER

clearance n. 清除. 空地. 空隙

+ item 清倉貨. 零碼貨

+ sale 用賣

500 West Main Street

178 Middletown, DE 19709

(852) 343-1243

*finish n.

1. 結束: The soldiers fought to the finish. 戰鬥到底

2. 拋光. 最後一道漆

3. (舉止, 談吐) 優雅
→ His manner lacks finish.
他的舉止欠佳

Mr. Lee Boatman
American Freight and Furniture Company
1920 Watterson Trail
Louisville, KY 40299

Dear Mr. Boatman,

我們兩週前收到床架,而且非常喜歡

We received our bed frame two weeks ago and are very happy.
We love the <u>finish</u> and the <u>quality</u> and it looks great in our
bedroom. We would like to know whether a matching set of
<u>night stands</u> could be built. We <u>looked through</u> your catalog
and liked the Mason Style shown on page 35. It matches our
bed frame but would be too large for the <u>limited amount of</u>
<u>space we have</u>. There is approximately two feet of <u>clearance</u>
on either side of the bed. The Mason is 24" wide; we would
need something closer to 18" wide. 24吋 inches

If this is at all possible, please let us know. Thank you very
much.

Richard & Lois Webber

1 呎 = 12吋, 1吋 = 2.54cm
1 foot = 12 inches
2 feet

FAX

in demand Good secretaries are always in demand.
She is in great demand as a singer. 受歡迎的歌手 ↓
好秒婚很

TO: D.W. McCall   Number: 502-355-6096
FROM: Lee Boatman   Number: 502-223-2396
需要

緊急 □ Urgent   檢查 □ For review   給意見 □ Please comment   請回覆 [X] Please reply （市場有需求）

Dear D.W.,
一組床頭櫃
I hope all is well in Cleveland. I just received a request from a family for a pair of custom night stands. They already have a bed frame in the Mason Style (on page 25 in our catalog) and would like smaller versions of the matching night stands (page 35). adj.足夠的,充分的 比較小的 版本 v.執行.完成.實現

Please let me know if you have sufficient time and materials to fulfill this order, and I will send their specific size requirements. I wanted to check with you first since I know your woodwork is in high demand. 受歡迎的.非常需要的
工.工 adj.特殊的.具體的

Thanks in advance. *refer ⑤提交: We referred the proposal to the board of directors.
①.提及
②查閱.參考 Please refer to the last page of the book for answers.
③涉及.有關 The rule refers to special cases.
④歸因: He referred all his troubles to bad luck.

Lee
americanfreight.us
+1 502-223-2396

176. What are Mr. and Ms. Webber requesting from Mr. Boatman? *B*
(A) Pre-assembled toys.
(B) Custom furniture. 客製化的傢俱
(C) Out of print books. 沒有樣本
(D) Used records. 使用紀錄

177. What is true about Mr. and Mrs. Webber? *B*
(A) They are living in a one-room apartment.
(B) They are satisfied with their purchase. 滿意
(C) They are concerned about the price. 關心價格
(D) They will order an item from a catalog. 從目錄訂貨

178. Where do Mr. and Mrs. Webber live? *B*
(A) Louisville.
(B) Middletown.
(C) Lexington.
(D) Paducah.

179. What is NOT suggested about Mr. McCall? *C*
(A) He is busy in his job. 可能沒有需要的材料
(B) He may not have the necessary materials.
(C) He has agreed to Mr. Boatman's request.
(D) He has worked with Mr. Boatman before.

180. In the fax, the word "fulfill" in paragraph 2, line 1 is closest in meaning to *A*
(A) complete. 完成
(B) appoint. 任命,指派,安排
(C) refer. 提及④
(D) search. 搜尋

GO ON TO THE NEXT PAGE.

From:	Noah Grist, Grist Produce 太陽山谷食品
To:	Carly Deal, Sunny Valley Foods
Re:	Order GP0711-98 PARTIAL SHIPMENT
Date:	September 6

①部分的 ②偏坦的 = She is partial | towards | to her youngest boy.
她偏坦小兒子

Carly,

如同以往. 謝謝你的生意。(和我們買東西)

As always, thank you very much for your business. I have sent via
已經藉由隔夜到貨快遞
overnight express four cases of Haas avocados to your store in Valley,
送了四箱酪梨到你在Valley的店
= Missouri 密蘇里   我們沒辦法送齊10箱給你
MO. Unfortunately, we could not send all ten cases of avocados you
因為   已經賣完了   你的訂單是最後的一筆
requested since they have sold out. Yours is the last shipment this
season from our warehouse in Modesto, CA. 是我們在Modesto倉庫這季最後一筆
這是我們第一次這麼快有項農產品賣完。
This is the fastest that we have ever sold out of any produce. This is
很有可能是由於   最近次版的文章   n.農產品
most likely due to a recent article published in Harvester Magazine in
我們果園視列在「加州最成功果園」之中
which our Table Rock Merced Orchard was featured among California's
果園   從那時開始
most successful orchards. Since then, we have had an unprecedented
number of orders. We are grateful for the attention, though we wish
我們很感激大家的注意   空前的
that we could better meet the demand. 雖然, 我們希望可以達到需求.(不要供不應求)
如果你仍想收到剩下的6箱
If you are still interested in receiving the remaining six cases of
請讓我知道   我有個朋友
avocados, please let me know. A friend of mine, Paul Shaffer, owns a
經營場所(一樣是水果的)
small operation called Pilot Orchard in Visalia and I could possibly get
you the remaining fruit.
剩下的   感謝各人的持續贊助 = 感謝各人一直回來
Thank you for your continued patronage and best wishes to you. 買東西.
n.資助. 贊助. 光顧
N. Grist

Grist Produce, Director of Operations   Under the patronage of sb.
某人的贊助下

*wonder
v. 想知道
n. 驚奇   adj. 非凡的

‹ Messages　　Noah Grist　　**Details**

↗賣酪梨的朋友 ，聽著，我剛賣完最後的酪梨，然後我還有幾個訂單要填滿（要完成）

Hey Paul,

How's everything at Pilot Orchard? Listen, I have just sold the last of my avocados and I still have several orders to <u>fill</u>. I'm guessing this has been busy season for you, too, but I was <u>wondering</u> if you have any remaining avocados that I can buy. <u>If so</u>, they can be sent to me at my warehouse. I will call you later today to discuss the payment and other details.

我猜這是旺季
但是我在好奇（想）你有沒有剩下的酪梨 可以跟你買

↳如果這樣的話（有酪梨的話）可以寄到
我的倉庫（Modesto）

今晚晚點打給你討論細節

Are you planning on attending next month's California Growers' Association meeting? It has been a while since we've had a meeting and it will be nice to see how everyone is doing.

I look forward ⟨to⟩ talking to you soon.

＊ preceding adj. 先前的 in the preceding chapter

＊前篇 produce 補充

produce v. 生產

produce n. 農產品

proceed v. 前進 著手 go

proceeds n. 收入 收益

proceeding n. 進行，聚會的會議紀錄

The proceedings were published in the newspaper.

precede 高於 優於，在…之前 go

precedence n. 優先權

precedented adj. 有先例的

181. What does the first e-mail indicate 指出 about Ms. Deal? 收件人

A

(A) She has ordered from Grist Produce before. 以前有跟他們訂過

(B) She works in California. 在加州工作

(C) She writes for Harvester Magazine. 幫 H 雜誌寫文章

(D) She owns an orchard. 擁有一個果園

依據

182. According to the first e-mail, what has affected the number of orders received by Grist Produce? 是什麼原因影響他們收到的

C (下)

(A) A change in shipping methods.

(B) Production of avocados at nearby farms. 鄰近農場

(C) Publicity provided by a magazine.

(D) A decrease in competition in the region. 這個區域的競爭變少

183. What does Mr. Grist offer to do for Ms. Deal? 確認另一位種植者是否有酪梨

A

(A) Check whether another grower has avocados.

(B) Issue a full refund. 發出全額退款

(C) Include her company in a magazine article. 把她的公司放在一篇雜誌文章中

(D) Fill the remaining order with a different item. 用不同的商品完成剩下的訂單

184. Where would Mr. Shaffer and Pilot Orchard send the order of avocados?

C

有酪梨園的朋友要把酪梨寄到哪裡

(A) To Visalia.

(B) To Valley.

(C) To Modesto.

(D) To Table Rock Merced.

如何討論價格?

185. How will Mr. Grist and Mr. Shaffer discuss the price of avocados?

B

(A) In person.

(B) Over the phone.

(C) At a meeting.

(D) By fax.

訂單數量

(A) 運送方法改變

(C) 雜誌帶來的宣傳效益

publicity
人工造

n. 宣傳、宣揚、公眾的注意

The new project gained publicity through papers.

* affect   v. 影響, 感動
to make, do

affection n. 情愛, 感情, 疾病

affectionate adj. 摯愛的

affectation n. 假裝
矯揉作勢

36

Questions 186-190 refer to the following article, schedule, and e-mail.

FINANCIAL GURU ON TOUR

New York (July 7) — Martha Leonard, one of America's most prominent financial advisors and owner of a financial services company for the past 20 years, will be giving a series of talks on various financial topics beginning one week from today.

On July 14, Ms. Leonard will speak at New York's Central Library. On July 15 and 16, she will speak at Chicago's McCormick Place Convention Center. On July 17, she will speak at Houston's City Conference Center. On July 18, she will speak at Denver's Memorial Library, and finally on 19 July, she will head to San Jose to give a talk at the McEnery Auditorium.

Tickets are limited. Visit www.leonardfinancial.com for prices and other information.

Martha Leonard's July Speaking Tour Schedule

City	Topic	Date	Time
New York	Mutual Funds – Emerging Trends & Funds	July 14	7:00
Chicago	Commodity Cycles in Emerging Markets	July 15	8:00
Chicago	Pension Maximization Using Life Insurance	July 16	7:30
Houston	Investing in Today's Economy	July 17	7:00
Denver	Commodity Cycles in Emerging Markets	July 18	7:30
San Jose	Traditional Cash Reserves	July 19	7:00

From:	j.lillard@leonardfinacial.com
To:	a.miller@technet.com
Re:	Martha Leonard Speaking Tour 巡迴演出
Date:	July 10

Inquire into 調查
about 詢問
for 求見

Dear Mr. Miller, 很不幸地,你詢問的在 Denver 的活動已經賣完了

然而,他會在7/15,於芝加哥演講相同的內容

Thank you for your interest in Ms. Leonard's speaking tour.
Unfortunately, the event you inquired about in Denver has already
sold out. However, Ms. Leonard will be giving the same talk in
Chicago on July 15, and that event presently has seats available.

adv. 2者擇一地,還有別的選擇   安排 目前還有可暑的位子

Alternatively, if you would like to set up an appointment with Ms.
Leonard to discuss her services directly via phone or
videoconference, I would be happy to arrange that for you.

視訊會議   我會很高興幫您做安排

Regards,

± tele conference   * engagement n. 訂婚, 諾言, 約會
電信會議   僱用

Jasmine Lillard

Leonard Financial

* arrange
  ə e

v. 整理, 安排.
she arranged the flowers
安排一個演說期.   In a vase.

186. What is indicated about Ms.
D Leonard?
   (A) She lives in Houston. library
   (B) She gives free talks at libraries.
   (C) She tours Europe every
       summer. 每年夏天遊歷歐洲
   (D) She has operated a business
       for 20 years. 經營一項生意20年了
       關於

187. Where will the talk regarding cash
D reserves be given?
   (A) At the Memorial Library.
   (B) At the City Conference Center.
   (C) At the McCormick Place
       Convention Center.
   (D) At the McEnery Auditorium.

188. What is the purpose of the e-mail?
C (A) To arrange a speaking engagement.
   (B) To decline an offer. 拒絕
   (C) To respond to a question. 回應
   (D) To confirm a change to a schedule.
       確認一個行程改變

189. What event date was Mr. Miller originally
C interested in?
   (A) July 16.
   (B) July 17.
   (C) July 18.
   (D) July 19.

190. What most likely is Ms. Lillard's job?
B (A) Graphic designer. 平面設計
   (B) Administrative assistant. 行政助理
   (C) Journalist. 記者
   (D) Ticket agent. 賣票等的人

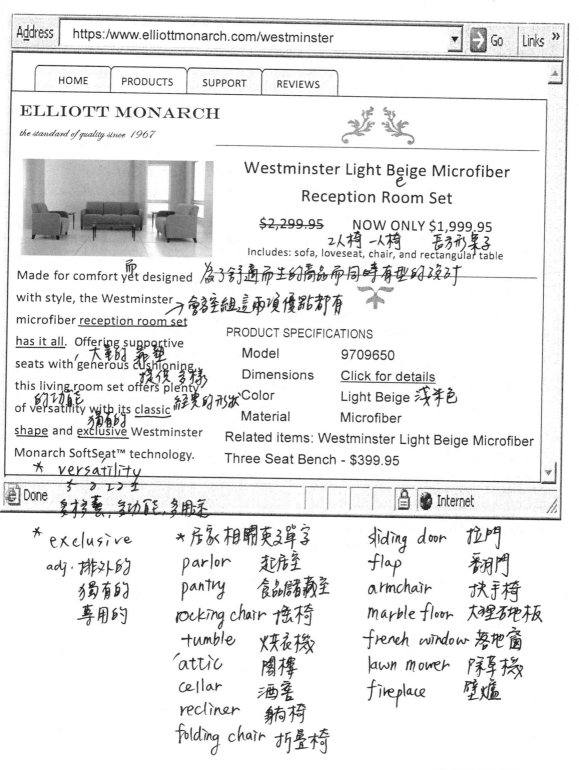

Address https://www.elliottmonarch.com/westminster   → Go   Links »

HOME   PRODUCTS   SUPPORT   REVIEWS

ELLIOTT MONARCH
the standard of quality since 1967

Westminster Light Beige Microfiber
Reception Room Set

~~$2,299.95~~   NOW ONLY $1,999.95

2人椅 一人椅   長方形桌子

Includes: sofa, loveseat, chair, and rectangular table

Made for comfort yet designed 為了舒適而生的高品而同時有型的設計

with style, the Westminster → 會客室組這兩項優點都有

microfiber reception room set

has it all. Offering supportive

seats with generous cushioning, 大量的 靠墊

this living room set offers plenty 提供多樣

of versatility with its classic 經典的形狀

shape and exclusive Westminster 獨有的

Monarch SoftSeat™ technology.

* versatility
多樣性, 多功能, 多用途

PRODUCT SPECIFICATIONS

Model   9709650
Dimensions   Click for details
Color   Light Beige 淺羊色
Material   Microfiber

Related items: Westminster Light Beige Microfiber
Three Seat Bench - $399.95

Done   Internet

* exclusive
adj. 排外的
獨有的
專用的

* 居家相關英文單字
parlor   起居室
pantry   食品儲藏室
rocking chair 搖椅
tumble   烘衣機
attic   閣樓
cellar   酒窖
recliner   躺椅
folding chair 折疊椅

sliding door 拉門
flap   翻門
armchair   扶手椅
marble floor 大理石地板
french window 落地窗
lawn mower   除草機
fireplace   壁爐

GO ON TO THE NEXT PAGE

HOME | PRODUCTS | SUPPORT | REVIEWS

ELLIOTT MONARCH
the standard of quality since 1967

Submitted by:
Dr. Roland Stevens
Stevens Family Physicians

Westminster Light Beige Microfiber Reception Room Set

practice — Dr. Pat is no longer in practice here.
n. 實踐. 練習. 慣例   沒在這裡執業了

nature 內科醫生   未以執業場所 (醫生.律師) →加州首府

I am a family physician with a private practice in Sacramento. I recently
重新裝修   接待處   診所   x x ε o
remodeled the reception area of my clinic. Most reception room furniture
light, raise
these days is uncomfortable, so it was a relief to find something that
強調舒適度大於功能性   n. 減輕. 放鬆. 和
emphasizes comfort over utility. I've been mostly happy with the
然而   直直   的→長方形)
Westminster Microfiber set; however, the rectangular table has caused
家庭從業人員
some problems. Because I'm a family practitioner, I see patients of all
ages. More than a few patients with children have raised concerns about
超過 一些(不只一些)有小孩的病人
the sharp edges of the rectangular table.

有提出擔心 關於這個尖銳的邊緣(桌子)   耐用度
I also have some reservations about the durability of this set. In
particular, the microfiber fabric has already shown signs of wear from
heavy use. This might be a problem in the long term.   n.① 磨損
長期而論是個問題   ② 耐久性

Done   🔒 🌐 Internet

我對於這組沙發的耐用度
有些保留態度 (意見.異議)   The sofa is showing signs of wear.
大其布料 (fabric) 已經出現使用   沙發有磨損的痕跡
磨損的痕跡。
                                 There is plenty of wear left in the machine.
✱ reservation   這台機器還可用很長一段時間
back keep
①佔有專用地 ②自然保護區 ③意見異議

ELLIOTT MONARCH

the standard of quality since 1967

151 BURLINGTON AVENUE, PALO ALTO, CA 94322
52834-0009

Dear Dr. Stevens,

We're sorry to hear about your trouble with our product. As a result of feedback like yours, we've introduced a new rectangular table with softer edges. If you contact us at: customersupport@elliottmonarch.com, we'll send you, in Light Beige, a duplicate of the table to complement your Westminster set. Note that this gift will be sent to you after you verify that you posted the online review.

We also hear your concerns about our microfiber technology. Rest assured that our lightweight fabric has been proven to withstand years' worth of rough treatment, maintaining its integrity after over 100,000 uses tested under stressful conditions in our laboratories.

Irene Coo, Elliott Monarch customer service

---

191. What does Dr. Stevens write about his furniture?
(A) He likes the color.
(B) The cushions are too soft.
(C) He purchased the set recently.
(D) The table injures his patients.

192. In the review, the word "durability" in paragraph 2, line 1, is closest in meaning to
(A) strength.
(B) force.
(C) size.
(D) intelligence.

193. What does Ms. Coo offer to Dr. Stevens?
(A) A full set of reception room furniture.
(B) A new sofa.
(C) A new loveseat.
(D) A new table.

194. What must Dr. Stevens do in order to receive a gift from Elliott Monarch?
(A) Retract negative feedback given on a website.
(B) Send a copy of his purchase order.
(C) Prove that he is the author of a product review.
(D) Complete a survey about new products.

195. What does Ms. Coo indicate about the table?
(A) It has been discontinued.
(B) It has been redesigned.
(C) It is out of stock.
(D) It is on sale.

GO ON TO THE NEXT PAGE.

41

Drexel Institute of Technology

Intermediate Craft Beer Brewing Course

CB-0002

Instructor: Joe Long

Cost: $150

This six-week course is designed to take the students on a journey through the world of craft beer. Each class will tap into a different area of craft beer. Some of the topics we will cover include the history of beer, the craft beer revolution, beer styles, beer and food pairings and many more. This course will serve as a general overview of craft beer and its role in today's culture. Intermediate Craft Beer will give you the foundation for all future courses in the program. If you don't already appreciate craft beer, you will when you have completed this course!

This course will expand on the introduction to brewing that is covered in CB 0001. Students will gain a deeper understanding of brewing terminology, as well as how the manipulation of raw ingredients and brewing practices result in the wide variety of beer styles. Our goal is to give students a stronger foundation in the art and science of brewing, so that they may serve the needs of the industry in a more thorough and insightful manner. The course will include a field trip to a local brewery. All course ingredients will be provided.

42

CB 0002 Course Description

拆穿12個釀酒迷思

Week 1 – Saturday, April 4, 9:00 a.m. 穀釀簡短概論

Short overview of grain brewing

The 12 myths of brewing dispelled 神話 =debunk =disproven

The 7 secrets to making good beer
7個做出好啤酒的秘密

Week 2 – Sat., April 11, 9:00 a.m.

All about Malt 麥芽介紹

Malting and Adjuncts

All about Hops /ˈædʒʌŋkt/ 附屬物
啤酒花 (酒香味、苦味從這裡來)

Week 3 – Sat., April 18, 9:00 a.m.

Yeast and Fermentation /ɪst/ n.發酵

Mashing 啤酒醣化   yeast 酵母

Designing a Beer

Week 4 – Sat., April 25, 8:00 a.m.

(Please note earlier start time)

Brew Day at Brady Brewery 釀酒廠

Lunch

灌注   裝瓶   裝桶

Week 5 – Sat., May 2, 9:00 a.m.

Hygiene, bottling, kegging and filtration 過濾

Home filtration

Water, oxygen pick up, oxygen ingress 進入, 入口

Week 6 – Sat., May 16, 10:00 a.m.

(Please note later start time)

Final exam 請注意開始時間比較晚

有多的釀酒時間, 週日9:00~17:00

Further Note: Additional brewing time at Drexel Institute is available on Sundays from 9:00 a.m. to 5:00 p.m. for those who would like more time with an instructor present. If you are interested in time with an instructor outside these hours, we recommend that you call ahead or be prepared to work independently.

如果你想在這時間以外約老師的時間
我們建議你事先打電話或是準備好要獨立作業
(不先預約可能沒老師)

NAME:	Joe Long

v. 發出, 配給, 流出

DATE/TIME:	March 30, 3:05 PM → Lava issued from the volcano.

Telephone	Fax	Email	Office Visit

199 他要上 CB0002 的課

MESSAGE:	Devin Yates called. He is taking CB 0002. He has a scheduling issue with the Brew Day trip and wondered if it would be OK for him to skip it. I told him that you would call him back to discuss it further. Please reach him at 595-8129.

訂程問題
＝行程衝突

在猶可不可以翻課

跳過

我跟他說你會回電給他做更進一步的討論

TAKEN BY:	Norm Smith

196. What is suggested about the brewing
A course? = to discuss a topic in more detail.
  (A) It will expand on a previous course. 更深入探討之前的課程
  (B) All ingredients must be purchased from the school. 材料要從學校購買
  (C) Students are required to be at least 18 years of age. 學生至少要18歲
  (D) It lasts five weeks. 持續5週

197. What does the course description
D indicate? 課程描述指出什麼
  (A) Drexel Institute recently expanded its parking lot. 擴展停車場
  (B) Instructors may reschedule a regular class to meet on Sunday.
  (C) Administrators invite suggestions for new classes. 熱請大家對新課提意見
  (D) Instructors can provide assistance outside of class time.
  老師在上課時間之外可以提供協助

198. In the brochure, the word "foundation"
D in paragraph 2, line 5, is the closest in
  meaning to 手冊   基礎
  (A) shelter. 遮蔽物, 家, 避難所
  (B) guarantee. 保證
  (C) material. n. 材料 adj. 物質的
  (D) basis. n. 基礎, 準則

199. What is most likely true about Mr. Yates?
D (A) He is under 18 years of age.
  (B) He works at Brady Brewery.
  (C) He is a master brewer. 釀酒大師
  (D) He has taken a previous course.
  有上過之前的課

200. To which class session does the
C phone message most likely refer?
  (A) Week 2.
  (B) Week 3.
  (C) Week 4.
  (D) Week 5.

Stop! This is the end of the test. If you finish before time is called, you may go back to Parts 5, 6, and 7 and check your work.

44

New TOEIC Speaking Test

Question 1: Read a Text Aloud

Directions: In this part of the test, you will read aloud the text on the screen. You will have 45 seconds to prepare. Then you will have 45 seconds to read the text aloud.

Come to Middletown Autos, the area's most trusted used

賣車商　　　不論你是在找　　　車, 禮車, 卡車, 廂型車

<u>car dealer</u>. Whether you're looking for a cár, <u>limo</u>, truck, or van,

有你愛的車　　　　　　　　　limousine

we have a vehicle you'll love. Plus, we guarantee that the cars

另外, 我們保證, 我們賣的車

we sell <u>are reliable</u> and that our prices are reasonable.

很可靠　　而且我們的價格很合理

Thousands of customers have trusted us, so make sure that

成千上萬(好好多)顧客信賴我們, 所以請確保

your next vehicle comes from Middletown Autos.

你的下台車是從我們這裡來的。(從我們這裡買的)

*(記) be V. 不會和 一般 V. 出現在 一起
✓ Where do you come from?　 ✗ Where <u>are</u> you <u>come</u> from?
　　　　　　　　　　　　　　　　　　　　　v.　　　v.
✓ Where are you from?

PREPARATION TIME
00 : 00 : 45

RESPONSE TIME
00 : 00 : 45

GO ON TO THE NEXT PAGE.

Question 2: Read a Text Aloud

5 ▶)) **Question 2**

Directions: In this part of the test, you will read aloud the text on the screen. You will have 45 seconds to prepare. Then you will have 45 seconds to read the text aloud.

行銷策略是你商業計畫中的一個環節,討論
Marketing strategy is a section of your business plan that
會繪出你整體全面計討的樣子。這個計畫就是你如何找到和吸引客戶
outlines your overall game plan for how you'll find and attract clients
有時行銷策略和計畫會
or customers to your business. Sometimes marketing strategy is
搞混   他們是不一樣的
confused with a marketing plan, but they are different. Your
策略   著重在   你的主意到達到什麼目標
marketing strategy focuses on what you want to achieve for your
可言   和行銷努力
business and marketing efforts. A marketing plan details how you'll
列出你如何達到這些目標的細節   包含
achieve those goals. A good marketing strategy incorporates what
如何讓你的生意高收入市場,(打入市場)   body
you know about how your business fits into the market and the
和行銷技巧及戰術
marketing techniques and tactics that will achieve your marketing
objectives.

STP   4P
Segmenting 市場區隔   Price
Targeting 目標市場   Product
Positioning 定位   Promotion
                       Place

行銷策略大方向計劃
↓
行銷計畫是細節執行

strategy
↓
plan
↓
implementation
↓
success

PREPARATION TIME
00 : 00 : 45

RESPONSE TIME
00 : 00 : 45

SWOT
Strength
Weakness
Opportunities
Threat

70

Question 3: Describe a Picture

((◖ 5 ◗)) **Question 3**

Directions: In this part of the test, you will describe the picture on your screen in as much detail as you can. You will have 30 seconds to prepare your response. Then you will have 45 seconds to speak about the picture.

PREPARATION TIME
00 : 00 : 30

RESPONSE TIME
00 : 00 : 45

GO ON TO THE NEXT PAGE

Question 3: Describe a Picture

答題範例

有些男人在排隊
Some men are <u>standing in line</u>.

他們可能試著要完成一種交易
They are probably trying to complete some kind of <u>transaction</u>.

It looks like a <u>government office</u> or <u>public institution</u>. A→B↑

看起來像政府辦公室或公家機關

Most of the men are waiting to <u>access</u> window 13. 大部分的人都想去

There's one man off to the side. 有個人到旁邊   13 號窗口

He's standing with his <u>arms folded</u>. 他雙手交疊站著

None of the other windows are open. 其他的窗口都沒開

包圍隔離
The line is <u>cordoned</u> off by some <u>stanchions</u>. 直立柱
Cordon   柱 子

It's impossible to say if there are any workers behind the windows.
窗口後有沒有人,不好說 (或不知道)

The man on the far left has a huge beer belly. 左邊遠處那個人

He's wearing glasses. 有戴眼鏡   有大的啤酒肚

He's at the end of the line. 他在隊伍尾端

One of the men in line is wearing a cap. 隊伍中有個男人戴帽子

The others have their backs (to) the camera. 其他人背對鏡頭

There appears to be a person standing next to the man who is at
window 13. 看起來有個人站在 13 號窗口前那人的旁邊

前景   有些工作人員坐在桌子前
In the foreground, a couple of workers sit at desks.

They don't appear to be doing any work. 他們看起來沒在做什麼工作

There's a bank of file cabinets on the left side.

有一堆資料櫃在左邊

Questions 4-6: Respond to Questions

 **Question 4**

Directions: In this part of the test, you will answer three questions. For each question, begin responding immediately after you hear a beep. No preparation time is provided. You will have 15 seconds to respond to Questions 4 and 5 and 30 seconds to respond to Question 6.

Imagine that a U.S. marketing firm is doing research in your country. You have agreed to participate in a telephone interview about public transportation.

Question 4

How often and for what purposes do you use public transportation?

Question 5

What is your experience with taxis and other types of car service?

Question 6

Describe one service or policy that you would like to be different about public transportation in your country.

RESPONSE TIME
00 : 00 : 30

GO ON TO THE NEXT PAGE.

Questions 4-6: Respond to Questions

答題範例

Question 4

多常,為何使用公眾交通工具?

How often and for what purposes do you use public transportation?

Answer

我每天都使用公眾交通工具

I use public transportation every day.

I take the bus to work. 我搭公車去上班

Then I take the subway to visit my parents.

然後我搭地鐵去拜訪我父母親

× expensive 只可以用來形容貴層的東西.

如要說:這個價格太貴了,價格是空虛的.不可用 expensive

→ The price is too low 低 , 房租 rent, 速度 speed 同理
high 高

🎧 6 **Question 5**

你搭計程車或是其他汽車服務的經驗是什麼?

What is your experience with taxis and other types of car service?

Answer

我偶爾搭計程車

I use taxis occasionally. 有些時候,我並無選擇

There are times when I don't have a choice.

up
Taxis are expensive but otherwise quite helpful. 除此以外

計程車貴,但除此以外蠻方便的(有幫助的)

Questions 4-6: Respond to Questions

efficient adj. 效率高的,有能力的
→ He is an efficient manager.

Question 6 → It's not efficient to hire poorly trained workers.

Describe one service or policy that you would like to be different about public transportation in your country.

僱用訓練不足的工人會防礙工作效率

Answer

台北有捷運 / 大眾的 迅速的 運輸

We have the <u>Mass Rapid Transit</u> (MRT) in Taipei.

It's very <u>efficient</u> and <u>dependable.</u> 效率高的且可靠的

It covers a lot of Taipei and New Taipei City.
運輸範圍涵蓋台北和新北市

我唯一的抱怨是捷運 12:20 就停止營運了
My only complaint is that it stops running at 12:20 AM.

當地的巴士也是大約那個時候停止
The local buses stop around the same time.

結束時間對我而言非常不方便
Ending service at that hour is very inconvenient for me.

很多人那個時間點(捷運收班時間)仍然在外面
Many people are still out in the city at that hour.

我們要咘未被迫早點回家或是搭計程車
We're either <u>forced</u> to go home early or take a taxi.

因此,我希望捷運 24小時營運.一週7天都開.
Therefore, I <u>wish</u> the MRT ran 24 hours a day, 7 days a

week. wish 希望,祝
hope 希望

Your wish is my command!

遵命?   命令

Questions 7-9: Respond to Questions Using Information Provided

set up
① 使～突出，使與眾不同 ／ 我有留下些時間盒報告
② 部，使用：I have set some hours apart for writing my paper.

🎧 **Question 7**

Directions: In this part of the test, you will answer three questions based on the information provided. You will have 30 seconds to read the information before the questions begin. For each question, begin responding immediately after you hear a beep. No additional preparation time is provided. You will have 15 seconds to respond to Questions 7 and 8 and 30 seconds to respond to Question 9.

analytical /ænˈlɪtɪkl/ adj. 分析的

analyze /ˈænl,aɪz/ v. 分析

analysis /əˈnæləsɪs/ n. 分析，解析

In the final / last analysis. 歸根結底

SET YOURSELF APART *(up)*

AMA Certificate Programs

$3,495 Save up to 56%! (哥斤)

想要增加你的專業名望和加速你的職業嗎？ ①加速 ②快速晉升

Want to increase your professional standing and fast-track your career?

經歷 知識　能力　 必要的技巧

Expand your <u>knowledge</u> and <u>capabilities</u> in one of the crucial skill areas below and earn an AMA Certificate—an <u>acknowledged</u> standard of achievement and excellence. Get your certificate by successfully completing 3 <u>designated</u> AMA seminars within 24 months.

指定的　傑出的　 我們公認代表成就+優良標準　認可的證照

What makes this new AMA Certificate program more <u>extraordinary</u>? You can now register for the three courses you need to earn your certificate and pay only **$3,495—a savings of up to 56%!**

分析技巧

Earn your certificate in:

ANALYTICAL SKILLS—applies to all levels

BUSINESS COMMUNICATION
Level 1—for high-performing professionals
Level 2—for managers and above

BUSINESS ESSENTIALS—for high-performing professionals

Financial Acumen—for newly-appointed managers
n. 精明，聰明

有抱負的領導者

LEADERSHIP DEVELOPMENT
Level 1—for aspiring leaders
Level 2—for experienced leaders

MANAGEMENT DEVELOPMENT
Level 1—for aspiring managers
Level 2—for first-time managers
Level 3—for experienced managers

PROJECT MANAGEMENT—applies to all levels

24個月內完成指定的 3個課程即可獲到證
acknowledge v. 承認
designate v. 指定，標明

For more information, email certificates@amanet.org or call your AMA Account Manager, 800-854-4493.

→和 business/politics 領域相關. 擅做決定/判斷

Hi, I'm interested in the AMA Certificate Program. Would you mind if I asked a few questions?

PREPARATION TIME
00 : 00 : 30

Question 7	Question 8	Question 9
RESPONSE TIME	**RESPONSE TIME**	**RESPONSE TIME**
00 : 00 : 15	00 : 00 : 15	00 : 00 : 30

Questions 7-9: Respond to Questions Using Information Provided

答題範例

《《6》》 Question 7

要花多久時間得到這個證照?

How long does it take to earn a certificate?

Answer

因人而異

It varies from person to person.

你必須完成3個課程在24個月之內

You must complete three courses within 24 months.

大部分的人可以完成課程在12個月或更短的時間

Most people can finish the program in 12 months or less.

《《6》》 Question 8

什麼讓這個證照顯得特別?

What makes this certificate program special?

Answer

首先,這個證照是廣泛認定成就的標準

First of all, the certificate is a widely recognized standard

of achievement. 成績.成就.達成

We're also running a promotional deal. 我們同時也在跑一個

Sign up now for three courses and save 56%. 推銷專案

現在登記上三堂課,省56% = 44折   (有打折)

GO ON TO THE NEXT PAGE.

*accountability
→ The fact of being responsible for what you do
and able to give a satisfactory reason for it /
the degree to which this happens.

《 6 》 Question 9

I'm interested in management development, but I don't have any experience.

Which level would be appropriate for me?

→ There should be accountability
in the management of funds.
應有人對資金管理承擔責任

→ To establish accountability
in the new government.
給新政府制訂出責任制度

Answer

管理發展課程有三個階段 (程度)

There are three levels of management development

courses.

有經驗的管理者
Level three is for experienced managers.

第一次當管理者的人
Level two is for first-time managers.

沒有經驗的人, 像你這樣
Level one for people with no experience, like yourself.

然而, 你可能打算申請管理職
However, you may plan on applying for a management

在不久的將來
position in the near future.

你就該選 Level 1
Level one is the program for you.

我們的證照提供一個扎實的管理基礎
Our certificate provides a solid management foundation.

你會明白這個職位的 可信性和責任.
You'll understand credibility and accountability (up)

你會學習到 如何把事情做好, 完成。
You'll learn how to get things done.

Question 10: Propose a Solution

 **Question 10**

Directions: In this part of the test, you will be presented with a problem and asked to propose a solution. You will have 30 seconds to prepare. Then you will have 60 seconds to speak. In your response, be sure to show that you recognize the problem, and propose a way of dealing with the problem.

In your response, be sure to

• show that you recognize the caller's problem, and

• propose a way of dealing with the problem.

PREPARATION TIME
00 : 00 : 30

RESPONSE TIME
00 : 01 : 00

GO ON TO THE NEXT PAGE

Question 10: Propose a Solution

答題範例

＊note
第記. 便條. 口氣 → His new theory is worthy of note.
他的新球論. 值得注意

((6)) **Question 10**

＊wrap up
Voice Message
完成. 結束. 包好. 總結. 概括

v. 摔角
Hey there, Michelle. This is George calling from Phoenix.
比賽剛結束 摔角錦標賽 wrestle , 比賽
Competition just wrapped up at the wrestling tournament here.
很不幸地 我們回家的班機延遲了
Unfortunately, our flight home has been delayed. I'm really
我很抱歉, 這代表著我不能夠到達區域 運動協會會議
sorry, but this means I won't be able to make it to the regional
運動的 協會. 公會. 社團, 聯想 What association do you have with
athletic association meeting tomorrow. I know you were the color green?
依賴我, 看著我 代表我們學校去開會
counting on me to represent our school at the meeting, and to
並且投票選出新的協會主席
vote for a new association chairperson. Do you think you
你覺得你可以代替我去嗎? 以好的方面來說
could go in my place instead? On a positive note, I'm very
up
我很高興 我們隊在錦標賽表現真好
pleased with how well our team did at the tournament. We
我們有6位選手在他們量級中得到前三
had six wrestlers finish in the top three of their weight class.
當我回去我再跟你說
But I'll tell you all about it when I get back.

Question 10: Propose a Solution

答題範例

Hi George, I got your message. 我收到你的訊息了

Sorry to hear that you're stuck in Phoenix. 抱歉聽到你卡在鳳凰城

But I'm happy to hear the wrestling team did so well! 但我很高興聽到摔角隊表現那麼好的消息

I could attend the meeting on your behalf. 我可以代表你參加會議

I might be a little bit late, though. 我可能會有一點晚到

I have to pick up my daughter from soccer practice. 我要去接我女兒練完足球

However, I need some information from you first. 然而，我需要先從你那裡問點資訊

Who were you planning to vote for chairperson? 你想投誰當主席

I'm not <u>familiar with</u> any of the candidates. 我對任一個候選人都不熟悉

Maybe I should abstain from voting? 也許我應該避開投票？（棄權）

That's your call. 你決定吧！ = You call the shot!

Let me know.

你是老大的說法

Anyway, great news about the team. 總之，關於摔角隊是好的消息
→ You are the boss.

They represented our school well. 他們飛好地代表了我們學校
→ You have the conn. v.掌舵 n.掌權

Please extend my congratulations. 請表達我的祝賀
→ You have the final say.

→ It's all up to you.

Return my call when you can. 你可以時請回電
→ You are in charge here.

Travel safe. 安全旅行. 旅行平安

Talk to you later. 再聯繫

GO ON TO THE NEXT PAGE

Question 11: Express an Opinion

《 5 》 **Question 11**

Directions: In this part of the test, you will give your opinion about a specific topic. Be sure to say as much as you can in the time allowed. You will have 15 seconds to prepare. Then you will have 60 seconds to speak.

Some countries enforce the death penalty on their worst criminals.

Do you support the idea or oppose it? Give reasons to support your answer.

有些國家強制對於最壞的罪犯執行死刑)
你支持還是反對呢?
給出理由支持你的答案.

PREPARATION TIME
00 : 00 : 15

RESPONSE TIME
00 : 01 : 00

Question 11: Express an Opinion

✻consequence
n. 結果, 後果

✻outweigh
v. 比~重要   答題範例

✻eliminate
v. 消滅, 排除

✻villain
n. 壞蛋

✻habitual
adj. 慣常的

✻harass
v. 騷擾

sexual racial | harassment

《🎧 6》 **Question 11** out

我完全支持這個想法
I fully support the idea.

最壞的罪犯應該被判死刑
The worst criminals should be put to death.

There is no reason to keep them alive. 沒有理由讓他們活著.   deter v. 嚇阻

死刑專於 嚇阻犯罪的觀念   制止, 制止物, 防碳物
The death penalty is based on the concept of deterrence of crime.

罪犯會被嚇阻, 如果犯罪的後果超過他的好處.
Criminals are deterred if the consequences of a crime outweigh the benefits.

Humans are basically aware of the differences between right and wrong.
人們基本上會意識到對和錯的差別

The commission of crime is a free choice involving choices based on consequences
of actions. 認罪是個自由選擇, 包含基於行為後果的選擇(要項)

The death penalty is an effective deterrence to criminals. 對罪犯來說死刑是個有效的嚇阻

The death penalty creates fear in the mind of potential offenders.
死刑可以在潛在的犯罪者(違法者)心中產生恐懼

The death penalty eliminates villains and habitual killers from the society who
would otherwise continue to harass people. 死刑會消除壞人和慣性殺手
當罪犯被處死了, 他就不再有行為威脅   在社會中會持續騷擾人的
When a criminal is executed, he no longer poses any threat.

This follows the logical argument that the execution of killers and other radical 極端的
offenders would contribute to safer societies. 這伴隨著是流合理的論點.

confine 限制
/rɪhə,bɪlɪ'teʃən/ 廣來殺手和其他極端的身犯者會導致更安全的社會
Confining criminals to prisons and rehabilitation centers involves expenditure of→ 常來
taxpayer money. 把罪犯關在監獄或是勒戒中心裡會花納稅人的錢

死刑的成本低 和牢年的大筆花費 相比
The costs of a death penalty are low compared with the enormous expenditure of jail.

There are also arguments that if the criminals are released, it may lead to panic and
fear in the society. 也有些論點是說如果罪犯放出來了, 可能會導致慌張和恐懼

除此之外   把罪犯關在牢裡會製造逃離拘留的可能性   拘留
In addition, keeping criminals in prisons creates the possibility of escape from custody.

This means that the individuals could commit more crime. 這代表著個個體(罪犯)會犯更多罪

The death penalty eliminates such possibilities of crime recurrence from the same
criminal. 死刑消除那樣的可能性
(同一罪犯再次犯罪)

GO ON TO THE NEXT PAGE.→

New TOEIC Writing Test

Questions 1-5: Write a Sentence Based on a Picture

Question 1

Directions: Write ONE sentence based on the picture using the TWO words or phrases under it. You may change the forms of the words and you may use them in any order.

library / cart

1. The cart contains books that belong to the library.
2. The man works in a library and uses a cart to return books to the shelves.

＊cart n. 推車 v. 粗野、強制地運送 → The police carted him off to jail. 押送

答題範例：**The man is pushing a library cart.**

GO ON TO THE NEXT PAGE →

Questions 1-5: Write a Sentence Based on a Picture

Question 2

Directions: Write ONE sentence based on the picture using the TWO words or phrases under it. You may change the forms of the words and you may use them in any order.

writing / table

The woman is writing on some papers on the table.

答題範例：**A woman is writing at a table.**

Questions 1-5: Write a Sentence Based on a Picture

Question 3

Directions: Write ONE sentence based on the picture using the TWO words or phrases under it. You may change the forms of the words and you may use them in any order.

player / judge

1. The player is arguing with the judge.
2. The player and the judge are having a conversation.

* judge n: 法官. 裁判員
        v. 判決. 評定 : Who will judge the case?

答題範例：**The player is complaining to the judge.**

You can't judge a book by its cover.
不能以貌取人

GO ON TO THE NEXT PAGE

Questions 1-5: Write a Sentence Based on a Picture

Question 4

Directions: Write ONE sentence based on the picture using the TWO words or phrases under it. You may change the forms of the words and you may use them in any order.

pour / coffee

The barista is pouring some coffee into a cup.
The man may be pouring some milk into the coffee.
* barista
  咖啡館服務生

答題範例：**The man is pouring some coffee.**

Questions 1-5: Write a Sentence Based on a Picture

Question 5

Directions: Write ONE sentence based on the picture using the TWO words or phrases under it. You may change the forms of the words and you may use them in any order.

man / shelf

The man is touching something on the shelf.
The man is most likely reaching for a bottle on the shelf.
*shelf n. 架子、暗礁 The ship hit a shelf of coral.
　　　　　　　船碰上珊瑚礁
shelf life 商品可以放在架上的時間
答題範例：**The man is reaching for an item on a shelf.**

GO ON TO THE NEXT PAGE.

Questions 6-7: Respond to a written request

智慧財產權 intellectual property rights

Question 6

adj. 智力的

intellect
inter | choose   選擇   n. 智力
between gather   取   理解力
read   讀

Directions: Read the e-mail below.

From: karen@cohen-scott.com

To: admin@onwardandoutbound.com

Subject: Photo usage 照片使用

Date: April 5

To Whom It May Concern,

My name is Karen Cohen-Scott, and I am an independent travel
我是個獨立的旅遊攝影師
photographer who owns a set of photographs that were improperly
我擁有一組照片   不恰當地
posted on your travel blog, Outward & Outbound. While I noticed
Do 在你的旅遊網誌上.   雖然 但盡管 注意
that I was properly credited as the photographer, your use of more
刻亥被 正確地 按到取材自我   你使用超過一張照片.
than one image violates my policy posted at
違反了我的政策. 貼在比網頁上
http://cohen-scott.com/usagepolicy. I am respectfully requesting
我恭敬地要求你
you remove these images immediately. 馬上移除這些圖片
然而 如果你願意付錢我會更高興
However, I would be more than happy, for a fee, to provide
photographs for your use. 可以提後照片後後使用

Thank you,
oversight
失案. 出錯
Karen Cohen-Scott   due to | an oversight
through

以旅遊部落格主的身分回信, 為疏忽出錯道歉, 並給出一理由
**Directions: Write back to Ms. Cohen-Scott as Reed Farber, owner of the
travel blog. Apologize for the oversight and give ONE reason
why you can't pay for the photographs.** 為何不能付費買照片

90

Questions 6-7: Respond to a written request

* pledge n. ③ 信物: Take this ring as a pledge of friendship.

①. 保證: I gave my pledge 答題範例 ④ 祝願: We drank a pledge that I would vote for him   to their success. 我們飲酒

Question 6 ⑤ 抵押(品): She left her watch as a pledge 祝願他們成功. with the taxi-driver.

Dear Ms. Cohen-Scott,

身為 OSO 的老闆   我誠摯對於不恰當使用您的照片道歉
As owner of Outward & Outbound, I sincerely <u>apologize for</u> the improper

+事 / apologize to + 人
use of your photographs on our travel blog. The photos have been

照片已被移除,我保證在未來會更加小心
removed and I <u>pledge</u> to be more careful in the future.

          OS O 在網路上出現才2個月
Outward & Outbound has been a Web presence for only two months and

而且我們每天一直加新內容進去   很準地,   在我們匆忙
we've have been adding new content daily. Unfortunately, in our haste to

推出我們品牌的同時,我們犯下一些錯誤   很明顯地   e 我們錯誤地
launch our brand, we have made several errors. Apparently, we wrongly

假設之前貼過po文的作者已經看過你的使用方針
assumed that the author of said post had read your usage guidelines.

因此, 我們沒有注意到你的使用政策和授權費用
Thus, we <u>were</u> not <u>aware of</u> your usage policies and licensing fee.

感謝   你的耐心而且   關於 這次的意外事件並尋求你的
<u>appreciate</u> your patience with us regarding this incident and ask your

原諒   當我們看到你的圖片時. 我們馬上認出(知道)
<u>forgiveness</u>. When we saw your images we immediately recognized their

這些照片的卓越品質 然而(但是),目前我們無法為這內容付費
exceptional quality. However, at this time we are unable to pay for content.

希望未來能購買您的 一些作品,當我們網站架設更好的時候
I hope to purchase some of your work in the future when our website is

並且有預算能夠付費買內容的時候
better established and we have a budget for paid content.

Sincerely,   * licence n. 執照 v. 發…許可證, 批準

Reed Farber, Owner/Founder * exceptional adj. 卓越的. 例外的

Outward & Outbound   貴族的

GO ON TO THE NEXT PAGE ➡

Questions 6-7: Respond to a written request

*名詞片語中有3個位置 限定詞→adj.→N.

可以把原本為N.的記改成adj.
就可以放在中間3
the most trusted name.

Directions: Read the e-mail below.

trust n.信賴
→ trusted 受信賴的

*severely
adv. 嚴重地
    嚴格地

From: Rodney Marchment
To: All Marchment Staff
Date: Thursday, July 23
Subject: Phone issues

To all supervisors and staff,

As you know, Marchment's is the most trusted name in electronics in the Sacramento area. However, our financial prospects continue to decline and it's time to shake things up. We have been in business for over 20 years. Just five years ago our annual sales were $75 million from our 12 stores, with two stores taking in over $15 million each. We all know that competition from big discount stores has severely cut into our sales. Consumers browse our merchandise but end up buying at the discount stores to save money. Even when we have major sales and match the discount retailers, people still buy from them. Last year's sales dropped to just $55 million dollars for our 8 remaining stores. If we can't reach sales of $60 million dollars before this year's end, we will be forced to close more locations. On the advice of my sister, an economist at Business Weekly, I am reaching out to all of you for feedback on how to increase sales and save our stores. Please e-mail me your ideas or call my secretary to arrange a meeting.

電子業棒頭

Thank you,

*reach out to sb.
→ to try to communicate with a person or a group of people

Stan Marchment
CEO
Marchment's Electronics

→ usually in order to help or involve them

*economist n. 經濟學者
    節儉的人

Directions: Reply to Mr. Marchment as Robin Watson, a salesperson with Marchment Electronics. List TWO problems and TWO possible solutions.

Questions 6-7: Respond to a written request

agonize v. 10分苦腦, 掙扎
→ agonized adj. 感到痛苦的

consolidate v. 合併
答題範例   統一

Question 7

Mr. Marchment,

我從公司開始就在這裡了,
I have been with the company since the very beginning, and as

音響部門的銷售人員, 我也是   被下降的銷售折磨著
salesperson in the stereo department, I too, have agonized over

我沒有大學文憑但是我認識到
declining sales. I don't have a college degree but I realize that if

如果我們不能和折扣店競爭, 我們將來會需要合併營業所
we can't compete with discount stores, we will have to consolidate

然而, 我可以指出2個重點, 我們會成為失敗
our operations. However, I can point to two areas of focus where

零售商的原因   第一, 大的折扣店有"無疑問退貨政策"
we fail as a retailer. First, the big discounters have "no questions

但是我們沒有,   有時人們買東西
asked" return policies — and we don't. Sometimes people buy

拿回家, 這不是他們想要的   甚至我的
something, get it home, and it isn't what they wanted. Even my

家人去折扣店買東西僅僅為了這個原因。   第二
family buys from the discount stores for that reason alone. Second,

我們停了我們 2手設備方案   是個一箭雙鵰的方案
we discontinued our used equipment program, which killed two

第一, 讓民眾以舊換新並
birds with one stone. First, it allowed people to trade in and

升級至更貴的商品   第二, 民眾可以購買
upgrade to a more expensive item. Second, people could buy

設備並知道, 可以用任何理由退還   因此
equipment knowing they could return it for any reason. Thus, they

民眾會更願意一開始時來這裡購買
were far more likely to make the initial purchase. Anyway, these

are only my suggestions.   *trade in
以舊換新的交易

Sincerely,

Robin Watson

Stereo Dept.

10th Street Store

GO ON TO THE NEXT PAGE

Question 8

Directions: Read the question below. You have 30 minutes to plan, write, and revise your essay. Typically, an effective response will contain a minimum of 300 words.

有時有個說法是. 從朋友那借錢會損吾友誼

It is sometimes said that borrowing money from a friend can harm

因此, 一個人向朋友借錢時要小心

or damage the friendship. Therefore, one must be careful when asking

寫篇文章, 用來描述怎樣借錢是最好的方法

a friend for a loan. Write an essay in which you describe the best way

包括具體的細節來解釋你的答案

to do this. Include specific details to explain your answer.

adj. 明確的. 具體的

※ 前面意 email 結語範例

謝謝幫忙

1. Thank you for your help / assistance / time / support.

2. I really appreciate the help / the _____ you've given me.

3. Thank you once more for your help in this matter.

請快回覆

1. I look forward to hearing from you soon.

2. I would appreciate your immediate attention to this matter.

3. please advice as necessary.

要更多資訊. 有聯繫我

1. If I can be of assistance, please do not hesitate to contact me.

2. If you require any further information, feel free to contact me.
   Should you need   ,

3. I hope the above is useful to you.

4. Let me know if you need anything else.

5. Drop me a line, if I can do anything else for you.

Questions 8: Write an opinion essay

*不管是借錢 or 借人錢者
常有欠會失去自己和朋友

Laertes 和 Hamlet 打架(比劍),不小心換劍後使自己中毒

答題範例

Question 8

向朋友借錢可以是個易等致失敗的狀況 (斜坡 有可能完全的改變這段

友誼 我們今都引用莎士比亞的話會考在裡面這句話是有原因的

Borrowing money from friends can be a slippery slope. It may completely change the relationship. There's a reason why today we still quote William Shakespeare's famous line from Hamlet, "Neither a borrower nor a lender be, for loan oft loses both itself and friend."

有些時候向朋友借錢是可被接受的

However, there are times when borrowing money from a friend is necessary and acceptable.

你要有穩固的友直
First of all, you must have a solid relationship with the person. An

一個相識的人或是某個你很少說話的人不是最好的借錢對象
acquaintance or someone you rarely speak to is not the best person to ask for a money

應該是個親近的,值得信賴的朋友,
loan. She or he should be a close, trustworthy friend with whom you would feel just as

這個朋友是若今天角色互換你也會覺得舒服的人
comfortable if the roles were reversed.

接下來,老實說 如果你對於為何需要這筆錢坦誠的說明 朋友會
Next, be honest. If you're truthful about why you need the money, a friend will

感謝你 你的 開誠佈公而且可能更傾向幫助你 同時,不要
appreciate your openness and may be more inclined to help you. Also, don't be

不好意思尋求建議 如果你向朋友借錢 你假設
embarrassed to ask for advice. If you are asking a friend for money, you are assuming

他們有資金 或心債 而且很可能看到他們是財務負責(財務沒問題
they have the funds to loan and most likely you see them as financially responsible. You

你也可以讓你的朋友看看你的財務狀況 並幫助你為出預算
may even ask your friend to look at your financial situation and help you create a budget.

這會給你的朋友保證(安心感)你不是草率地做出這項要求 草率地
This gives your friend the assurance that you're not taking this request lightly.

第三 不要把朋友的慷慨視為理所當然 即使你朋友是眾所皆知
Third, don't take your friend's generosity for granted. Even if your friend is known for

的大方 你仍還不該利用那個事實,除非你真的陷入困境
being generous, you should never take advantage of that fact unless you're genuinely in

你可能考慮把你的要求寫下來 列下你要借的金額和你
a bind. You might consider putting your request in writing. State the amount you wish to

還錢的日期 借款應該被嚴肅對待,而且
borrow and the date you will pay the loan back. The loan should be taken seriously and

追蹤 就像是 和銀行借錢一樣
tracked as if it were a loan from a bank. Keeping a good record will help prevent any

保持好的記錄會幫助防止過程中引起的怨恨
resentment during the process.

尤其,你應該在你有自信可以還并的情況下才借錢 *crucial 重要的
Above all, you should only borrow money if you're confident you'll be able to pay the

如果需要,言明息最好 你能做到你口頭/書面的承諾是很重要的
friend back—with interest, if necessary. It's crucial that you meet the terms of your verbal

不要出賣你朋看出你出門,欠了更多債或消費購買,可能出現
or written agreement. Do not go out and incur more debts or purchase things that may

浪費出的樣子 在敗 你在眼這些方對
come across as wasteful expenditures in the eyes of your friend. With these guidelines in

mind, you should be able to borrow money and still maintain a close friendship.

你應該可以借錢.同時仍維持一段親密的友誼

95